"Sybil Edwards—a professor giving advanced English conversation and film classes at the United Nations—knows how to keep a secret; she's spent years hiding the physical scars of a barbaric medical battle. But her teaching assistant, Laryssa, is hiding something far more dangerous: a past working for an autocrat and a present connected to the highest levels of the Kremlin.

As Russian forces move through the Belarusian corridor, the two women are propelled from New York into a high-stakes investigation of war crimes and international espionage. Blending chilling contemporary facts with a heart-pounding fictional chase, *My Friend the Spy* explores the "chiaroscuro" of the human soul. In a world of master spies and double agents, Sybil must uncover the truth about her friend before the clock runs out on Plan B."

—Saulius Kondrotas, author of *Gaze of the Viper*

"[T]he procedural elements, from Laryssa's covert operations and strategic planning to her work within Belarusian and international intelligence networks, providing an authentic view of spycraft . . . is informed and meticulous. The settings are as fully fleshed out as Seret's characters, whether it's bustling cities, serene gardens, or the jungles of Mexico. . . . Every mission, conversation, and observation contributes to a read that is exciting, intelligent, and satisfying, and I look forward to seeing what Seret comes up with next. Very highly recommended."

—Asher Syed, *Readers' Favorite*

"What makes *My Friend the Spy* particularly compelling is Roberta Seret's ability to blend fact with fiction, infusing the narrative with real-world geopolitics, Belarus's dark complicity in Russia's war, and the inner lives of women working in the shadows of autocracy. . . . It felt like reading a story taking place on the contemporary political stage."

—Romuald Dzemo, *Readers' Favorite*

"Based on real political events, the novel explores how personal relationships survive under pressure and whether individual conscience can resist state violence. Part spy story, part political reflection, *My Friend the Spy* reminds us of the importance of truth, art, and humanity in times of war."

—Martynas Ivinskas, Counsellor for Lithuania and European Union in Brussels

"[T]he writing has a lovely, dreamy quality, and references to Proust's madeleines, the psychological drama film *Tár,* and the works of Chagall and Picasso add depth to the narrative. . . . A lyrical and moody work."

—*Kirkus Reviews*

MY FRIEND THE SPY

Cherry
Orchard
Books

MY FRIEND THE SPY

ROBERTA SERET

CHERRY ORCHARD BOOKS
2026

Library of Congress Cataloging-in-Publication Data

Names: Seret, Roberta author

Title: My friend the spy / Roberta Seret.

Description: Boston : Cherry Orchard Books, 2026.

Identifiers: LCCN 2026002078 (print) | LCCN 2026002079 (ebook) | ISBN 9798887198941 (hardback) | ISBN 9798887198958 (adobe pdf) | ISBN 9798887198965 (epub)

Subjects: LCGFT: Spy fiction | Novels | Fiction

Classification: LCC PS3619.E744 M9 2026 (print) | LCC PS3619.E744 (ebook)

LC record available at https://lccn.loc.gov/2026002078
LC ebook record available at https://lccn.loc.gov/2026002079

ISBN 9798887198941 (hardback)
ISBN 9798887198958 (adobe pdf)
ISBN 9798887198965 (epub)

Book design by Kryon Publishing Services
Cover design by Ivan Grave
Editor: Marcia Rockwood
Photo ©: Roberta Seret

Published by Cherry Orchard Books, an imprint of Academic Studies Press
1007 Chestnut St.
Newton, MA 02464, USA
press@academicstudiespress.com
www.academicstudiespress.com

Contents

In Appreciation

No book is written alone.

Words and thoughts come alive on the page only after they are shared with those the author respects. I've been fortunate to have family and friends who've believed in me. For without them, this book could not have taken shape.

My deepest appreciation to each one of you:

Daniel Frese, PhD, Acquisitions Editor, Slavic Studies, Academic Studies Press; Marcia Rockwood, my insightful editor; Mridula Agarwal, my tech Guru; and Sanem Altayli, an artist with vision.

My family and friends: Ira and Sylvia Seret; Judith Vogel; Gaby Ciarlo; Lydia Eviatar, MD; Katia Tinajero; Vivian Haime Barg; Solvita Denisa-Liepniece; Ritva Metso; Martynas Ivinskas; and Saulius Kondrotas.

My sons: Greg and Cliff.

And my husband, Michel, always at my side, with his joie de vivre and optimism.

Thank you all,

Roberta

Untitled, charcoal on paper. Used with permission of the artist, Sanem Altayli.

For Michel

My best friend, the squirrel, and I, the mouse, took a bike ride through Central Park. Two paths crossed our way.

"Which one should we take?" squirrel asked me.

We eyed each other and answered as one.

"The path that tempts with twists and turns, ups and downs, rocks and brush, yet full of flowers."

"Are you strong enough to climb the hill?" He smiled at me.

"Yes, and I'm not afraid if I'm with you."

"I see the sun. Let's go seek what's Beyond."

We rode on, together, searching for secrets and finding truths.

Author's Note

Dear Reader,

My fascination with politics and history finds its influence in my work at the United Nations (2001 to the present) where I have created an NGO (international Cinema Education) to show students foreign films that teach global events.

My interest in film extends to literature with several of my historical novels. They share a style of blending fact with fiction to narrate stories in a hybrid fashion. The facts in *My Friend the Spy*, are true, using the politics of Belarus as my central theme. The fiction, however, is a creation of my imagination, where I interweave fictional characters with events of the day. These literary characters are not based on any living person. They serve as seeds to ignite creativity and emerge as political figures on their own. They are all products of my fantasy—except for the narrator, who sometimes resembles me.

Roberta Seret, PhD
New York City
November 3, 2025

PART 1

NEW YORK CITY

September 2022 to February 2023

A symbol of non-violence at the United Nations, New York City.
Photo courtesy of the author.

CHAPTER 1

A Friendship of Secrets

Engines soften as the New York Ferry navigates the East River. Thick fog coming from the north folds Manhattan into an entity of its own. The Triboro Bridge has disappeared, lost in soft layers of clouds.

As I study my city, it's hard to decipher where the ferry is heading. Only memory can tell me we're nearing the rectangular building of the United Nations where I've taught for twenty years. The angular lines of the Secretariat edifice are now obliterated by haze, lost to sight. The city appears mysterious.

I prepare to disembark; the fog surrounds me. Shadows and shapes of a city threatened by weather overcome me. Only habit helps me proceed as the whistle shrills and the ferry stops.

I'm thinking of the person I will soon meet for lunch. As I follow the trail through the park to First Avenue, I try to visualize Laryssa. But her face gets lost in my mind. Like shadows of chiaroscuro, parts of her features are unclear and abstract. The Russian high cheekbones, blue slanted eyes, face of pale complexion and pointed chin, all appear to me like a Cubist rendering of reality. Only her long, curly red hair the color of roses that flow across my Zoom screen each week, is overwhelmingly clear. I visualize her manicured fingernails, the same rose color. They flutter about like red cardinals, while she chats in my class.

But now I can only see one feature at a time, isolated from another, angles askew on different planes, in strange locations from where they should be. I close my eyes tight, hoping to assemble the parts so that they create a whole. But they remain in my mind, abstract. Elusive. Perhaps if I concentrate on something concrete about her, I'll be able to piece together the puzzle of her face.

Laryssa Pavlovich, Russian-born, having grown up in Belarus, has been my Teaching Assistant for two years at the United Nations where I've been teaching a class of Advanced English conversation and Film. She has been assigned to me by the Language department, but often, she's absent.

"Business," she kept saying, when she excused herself for missing many Zoom classes last semester. "My husband and I will stay overnight outside the city . . . in Washington D.C. . . . I help him, with business meetings."

What kind of business, I wondered. Her husband is a general, a military attaché to the United Nations, and she had never studied business or Finance. After finishing high school, she relocated from St. Petersburg to Minsk, the capital of Belarus, to study broadcasting and international relations at the university. Belarus, as an eastern European country in transition at that time, had a more open-door department in foreign affairs than her homeland, Russia. Her doctoral dissertation on conflict resolution became a textbook source for students of foreign policy. Immediately afterwards, she remained in Belarus and entered the ministry's administration. There, she worked for fifteen years as a broadcaster for their Russian-language television channel. She was also appointed Director of Television-Media for the president's office. And then . . .

Rumors abounded as the dictator, Lukashenko, was frequently seen with his glamorous media assistant. She was even referred to as the "Red Rose of Belarus," and has been considered a potential successor to the dictator-president, given her cunning and brilliance.

But what business, I kept thinking—for Belarus, in the middle of the most ferocious war since World War II—Ukraine's and Russia's horrific war. A war that has involved all Europe. All the world.

And why Washington? Is her business government related? Pentagon related? Clearly, her husband works for the military. I was so intrigued!

I kept telling myself to search for the reason in what she was doing. I could not accept that she was not involved, somehow, in helping her country or being part of this war. Conflict resolution, that was her specialty. Her dissertation. She must be working to solve the greatest political conflict of her time. How could she not?

There must be a solution to all this horror of war, to the destruction of millions of lives, thousands and thousands killed and maimed, countless number of limbs from innocent people amputated, cities reduced to rubble, people living without heat, electricity, water, food. There have been thousands of Ukrainian children kidnapped and taken to Russia. UNICEF claims that these abducted children are listed on adoption websites—being sold. And Belarus is part of it.

Belarus is Russia's dark and secret accomplice. Putin's goal is to wipe away the existence of Ukraine. To make the Ukrainian children Russian is just one of his means. Belarus's dictator helps him. I hoped she'd find an answer—a way to resolve this horrific disaster of inhumanity and crimes.

I had to read between the lines while talking to Laryssa. She usually answered me with a shrug and frozen grin, responding with a common mantra, "I'm at the UN with my husband and we have to concentrate on the interests of our country."

I wondered what was true. Could Laryssa tell me something positive about all this horror of human suffering? Would Laryssa's words be enough to forgive her in my mind for working with Lukashenko?

In my imagination I saw Laryssa's lips separate in the air. It reminded me of a painting Picasso did of his mistress, Dora Maar, depicting an abstract mouth that could not talk straight.

I continued walking and thinking, following First Avenue. The warm September air mixed with a cold northerly wind from the East River. Lost in my thoughts, walking with my head downward, I suddenly heard the piercing sound of an ambulance. Looking up, I focused on my surroundings. The fog had lifted. I saw an opening in the sky, a ray of sunlight giving me a sharper view of the UN structure and a path ahead. I continued walking more comfortably through the park.

Who was this Laryssa Pavlovich that I was going to meet in person for the first time—not only an image on my screen that I had seen for months? COVID had isolated me from my students, keeping me active only digitally. And yet, as my Teaching Assistant, she had taken the initiative through the screen to become a participant in my class and had emerged as the most talkative member. "Film," she had told me, "is my passion."

What did I know about her? Her registration papers told me that she was the wife of the military attaché of Belarus, a small country of nine million people in northern Europe that was not a member of the European Union or NATO. A landlocked country bordering on Russia, Ukraine, Poland, Lithuania, and Latvia. It was little known until the Ukrainian war, and its dictator became Russia's "marionette."

Curious, I had done some research. Belarus is a mystery to many, and yet, its dictator, Alexander Lukashenko, known as Sasha to his friends and family, and Batia (father) to the public, is very well known to Vladimir Putin. Brothers, they call themselves.

How linked is Laryssa to these two autocrats? A general is chosen by the country's defense minister, who is chosen by the president. Did her husband, the general, as well as Laryssa, share common values with these dictators? Did they look away as these leaders arrested anyone who disagrees with them? As they destroy dissidents to a murdered silence?

From our Zoom screen, Laryssa appeared narrow-shouldered and thin. I couldn't guess how tall or short she was, or what her body language revealed of her character as she talked. Yet, I could sense her aggression and passion. There was something cold about her. Was it ambition? Was she the type of person who could risk everything to succeed no matter what the cost? Did she have such a strong ego to think that no one would learn of her schemes? Was it conceit or obsession? Was she good or bad?

She appeared to be about fifty years old, very beautiful, extremely charming, and quite sure of herself. She wore hanging pearl earrings that dangled from her fiery red hair. Every week she wore another style of black sweater, and her red manicured fingernails would cover the screen in a flutter with her questions and comments.

Even through my computer, I could feel there was something dynamic about her. Nothing could stop the fire in her from bursting through the screen. I was intrigued to know what was behind the protected image. I felt compelled to find out—to figure her out. How could I not be? I love novels, film, literature. Am I really living in a spy story?

I'm driven to solve enigmas. What could be more mysterious than this woman appearing before me on Wednesdays for two years? So different from anyone I have ever known. And I wondered—was this woman a link to a war that had no heart, no soul, no logic? Was she a reflection of this war? Influenced by it? Was there more to her than the intrigue emanating from my screen?

Chance had brought this woman to my class at a time when history was in the making. How could I not want to study her and her story?

I had a unique opportunity known only to me: to uncover what was in front of me—a mysterious woman who was possibly involved in the most horrific politics of our time. During our Zoom classes, she was always alone in her apartment with her computer at a simple wooden table, talking in heavily accented English, concentrating on her thoughts without caring about her words.

Sometimes I recognized that the background behind her was in New York City; sometimes she was in her capital city, Minsk. In both cities she appeared far away, isolated in her own world in front of my screen. And I wondered if there was a rationale to her chatting with no one near. Did she have the need to talk? She was opening herself up to me. Liberating herself from . . . I didn't know what . . . Perhaps the computer and I were mere pretexts for her to do so. She had her reasons not to feel alone—to not be judged as wrong. I sensed she wanted me to see the good side of her—the intelligent side.

I was the professor—guiding the conversation with a person who had been assigned to help me with my class; a person who probably had never been controlled, despite growing up in controlling countries. Did I want to shatter her control? What did I want from the scattered pieces?

I asked myself if I was trying to force my subject matter of film into the realm of reality. By studying her, I was attempting to bring fiction to fact. To document real political subjects as a way to plant them in my written pages and nurture them like my private garden. I had always dreamt of writing a spy thriller and using politics to reveal human truths and the complexities of human behavior.

I wondered if it was a rationalization to tell myself that fate had chosen me to tell this story. My hope was that my circumstances were not a coincidence; this was not merely chance.

How did I end up working at the United Nations—with Laryssa, unknowingly, guiding me to write my spy novel?

* * *

In 1992 I broke my right arm. Within twenty-four hours, my arm was diagnosed as a pathological fracture, broken at the site of a tumor. To determine if the tumor was benign or malignant, a biopsy had to be performed. My husband—a doctor—asked his colleague, an orthopedist, after several preliminary X-rays were taken, what the prognosis would be if the biopsy found that the tumor was malignant?

"Not good," I heard the colleague whisper. "It could be a very rare angio-sarcoma which would entail amputation followed by intensive chemotherapy. Hopefully, that would save your wife's life." After overhearing such a death sentence, my mind went into shock. I was not able to think or feel.

Each day for a week my indefatigable husband took me to another specialist. No one had ever seen such a case before. We went from one chief of orthopedics to another, from one oncologist to another, from one surgeon to another.

"Amputate the arm" they all concurred. "That's the only chance to save her life. You must choose—her arm or her life."

How is this happening to me, I thought. I'm young. I don't smoke. I don't drink. Never took drugs. Why? What should I do? I have two teenaged sons, a loving husband, a successful career. A beautiful life. Don't take my arm!

More tests. More doctors. They were all so kind. Too kind. This must be very serious. Everyone is too nice. It's one of those bad cancers. I googled it: only five cases in America that have been documented. Prognosis: not more than five years of life.

My poor husband.

What happened to me during those early months of cancer? I chose to keep my arm. I was lucky my husband found two doctors at his hospital who were visionaries. I would become their guinea pig.

I took the risk. The treatment: experimental surgery. Surgical removal of the rotator cuff and shoulder, along with adjoining muscles, cartilage, tissues, nerves, capillaries. Replacement of the right humerus and shoulder with a cadaverous bone and prosthesis. Intensive chemotherapy for six months.

My oncologist was Dr. James Holland, eminent chief of oncology at Mt. Sinai Hospital. A genius. As he said, "Guinea pigs live. They're too valuable." But what he did not say was how much they would suffer.

"I am going to give you more chemotherapy than I have ever given anyone else." He made it sound like something special.

I felt as if Dante's descent into hell was nothing compared to mine. An inferno which began with the first round of chemotherapy that put me into a coma, followed by multiple allergic reactions. The chemotherapy had been too powerful. Then there were months when the lining of all my skin layers was burned by the poisons they pumped daily into my portacath.

The lining of my esophagus, windpipe, larynx, and mouth were all burnt to a crisp. Food could not pass through my charred throat. Excessive weight loss, continuous vomiting; I had a zero count of red and white blood cells. Dozens of blood transfusions. I lost all my hair. A barbaric treatment. I had become a medical experiment.

But the guinea pig lived. The prognosis was that I had to adapt with a rigid, non-functional right arm and shoulder that aesthetically, was thinner and stiffer than the left arm. Close scrutiny would make it appear odd. A very small price to pay.

I had to adapt to a new life. I began first with work: previously, I had been director of relocation at the New York Chamber of Commerce. It was a stressful job as consultant, lecturer, writer. I would have to find an alternative with less stress, less *angst*. Work would have to be my therapy.

Next, I would have to compromise in my personal life: I had changed, physically. I had limitations. My right arm was there aesthetically, but not functionally. In order to eat, I became a lefty. In order to function, I had to depend only on my left arm. I also had to spend months learning how to hold my right arm without it hanging limply at my side. My secret goal was to shake someone's hand naturally while saying hello. My trick was to move forward several steps and achieve an abduction of several degrees to be able to move my right hand and shake another's without being detected as struggling. And there were also my two teenaged sons. I did not want them to view me as disabled.

It took three years of physiotherapy and hard work to achieve my physical goals of appearing normal. My hair grew back, curlier than before, but very cherished, and I found another path of work: I returned to teaching, in just the way I had begun my career after grad school. Chance, or God, offered me a ray of hope. A friend at the UN said the English language department was looking for a teacher for diplomats who wanted to improve their language skills.

I jumped at the opportunity, despite the fact that ESL was a different type of subject matter for me to teach. At the same time, I created an NGO at the United Nations: International Cinema Education. I would use film to teach inner-city students about world affairs by screening foreign cinema at the UN Dag Hammarskjold Theater. Ambassadors would be their hosts for the question and answer sessions.

I wanted to give back for my being able to live. I decided that film and teaching would be my vehicles.

My diplomatic students enjoyed the different approach of using film to converse in English. The films were screened in the original language and the English subtitles served as vocabulary lessons—especially for the slang. The films came from all over the world and sometimes, from my students' own countries. Their insights and experience were invaluable lessons for all of us. I believed that I was the one learning the most from my diplomats, allowing me their friendship and opening my imagination by traveling.

After twenty years of teaching, I found myself with a Teaching Assistant who had a lot in common with me: we were two women with secrets. She did not know about mine—medical—of barbaric chemotherapy; and I did not know about hers—political—of barbaric human suffering. But there was a certain electricity in the air when we spoke together. A communication that went beyond words, perhaps from our life experiences. Or from our secrets. I was the one who became inquisitive first.

Laryssa, wife of the general from Belarus, had been my TA for two years when the war in Ukraine exploded on February 24, 2022.

Laryssa . . . the name in Russian meant citadel, fortress, *protection.* Is that the way she wanted to see her role as a general's wife—a stronghold protecting her nation? Sometimes I got the impression that she was an actress who thought that nothing would be her fault for following the rules of her dictator-president. She kept saying, "I'm just doing my job at the United Nations."

She had many roles, and her life for me was a stage—a stage to put in my book.

I sensed the role she feared the most was to be found guilty of crimes against humanity. I wanted to find out why.

CHAPTER 2

Waiting at the United Nations; My Personal Détente

I approached the UN security guards at the main gate on First Avenue and 46th Street. Showing my badge, I proceeded through security toward the square of the Secretariat building's outdoor plaza. The weather was still hazy and appeared to coalesce inside the square. I walked slowly and then paused in front of my favorite sculpture of a gun with its long barrel twisted, so the revolver would never be able to fire. Strangely, the fog from the East River shrouded the gun—the fog of war I thought, and a slight chill went through my body.

I waited for Laryssa. I was always early for any appointment. I reasoned that I would have some time to learn about the person while I was waiting for her, and also to learn more about her dictatorial boss.

I was wondering about Laryssa's opinion on this war—where did her allegiance lie—towards Russia or to the West?

Suddenly, my cell phone rang. I was startled from my thoughts. Then I realized it was Laryssa.

"Professor, I'm so sorry. I'll be late—so unlike me."

She spoke in a low tone, slightly hesitant as if someone was near or she was afraid.

"Can you wait for me. I'll be there."

"Yes. How long will you be?"

"I'm not sure," she whispered. "But I'll be there." She didn't sound like her usual confidant self.

"No problem. I'll wait."

Since I had time, I thought I would look a bit more into Belarus. I took off my locket—a Mother's Day gift from my husband, Gene, and my two sons. It was a large silver heart that I wore around my neck on a silver chain. When opened, one half of the heart has a photo of my three men, smiling at me. The other half has Google capability. I used this application when I wanted to be inconspicuous, as I did now, standing amidst cameras at the UN. But the maps and images were blurred. The size of the words was small, and I wanted to see them more clearly. Not wanting to put on my eyeglasses, I closed the locket, returned it to my neck, and taking out my phone, googled Belarus. I wanted to see the map more clearly, and also learn more than I could recall.

Belarus, a small Eastern European country, located between Ukraine and Russia, has a modest population of nine million people. In the past ten years, Belarus has come into the international forefront because of its submissive alliance with Russia and its strategic location to Ukraine.

On February 24, 2022, it was from Belarus that Russian troops began their invasion of Ukraine. Putin reasoned that it was easier to invade Kyiv from the Belarusian corridor than from Russia. Without wavering, Putin ordered his soldiers with their artillery, tanks, planes, missiles and drones, to attack Ukraine from Belarusian soil. Its dictator, Lukashenko, allowed his country's territory to become a ruthless launching pad and Putin's scapegoat.

What people don't know is that Putin had meticulously planned the invasion, months before February 24. Media has indicated that on February 7, 2022, from the shipyard at Hamburg, Putin had his favorite yacht, the Graceful, sailed from Germany, where it was undergoing repairs, to safer Russian waters.

He had told the harbor master in Hamburg that he wasn't satisfied with the progress of renovation, and he wanted the yacht sailed to Kaliningrad, in Russian territory on the Baltic Sea, where the repairs could be completed.

With two shifts of crew, sailing night and day, the yacht arrived at the port of Russia's Kaliningrad, just days before the invasion of February 24. This saved Graceful from being impounded by international sanctions.

Putin also planned to start his invasion of Ukraine after the winter Olympics in Beijing. Dictator-President Xi Jinping wanted to preserve the façade of Olympian peace and brotherhood, so he conferred with his ally, Putin, to wait until after the closing ceremony. That was held in Beijing on February 20, 2020. Putin attacked Ukraine four days later on February 24.

He had listened to Xi.

The day after Russia's invasion of Ukraine from Belarusian territory, on February 25, Putin continued his meticulous planning. He made sure that his ally, Lukashenko, would be properly compensated for his territorial assistance.

On that day, a private, unregistered Russian construction company began building a luxury residence for Lukashenko in the mountains near Sochi. Architectural plans for the palace were approved that included Turkish baths, two swimming pools, a movie theater, clay tennis courts, a massage room, fitness center, hotel, and restaurant. The luxury complex on twenty-four acres was designed to be Lukashenko's kickback. It could serve as his new home after he leaves office . . . either voluntarily or forcibly.

I googled further—this time to learn more about the person I was waiting to meet. I had time, Laryssa was late, and I was growing more and more curious.

A photo of Laryssa popped up with her and the dictator. They were standing close together, chatting and laughing. He was leaning toward her, as she remained straight and upright, keeping him at bay. The caption read: LUKASHENKO WITH HIS MEDIA SECRETARY, LARYSSA PAVLOVICH.

Surprised, I took another look, enlarged her face, stared at her blazing red hair, her sculpted face and high cheek bones. Was it Laryssa, my Teaching Assistant? I wasn't sure. The photo was at least fifteen years old. I left Google and went to my phone's documents to check my class roster. I verified the spelling of her name—Laryssa Pavlovich. I checked her photo next to her cell number. It had to be her!

I returned to Google. Searched more. She was on Wikipedia. More photos, the same red curly hair. No one had hair like that. It could only be her! I found an article entitled "THE RED IRON LADY." The article began by stating, "Everyone knows about Laryssa Pavlovich in Belarus." Immediately after graduation from the university of Minsk, Laryssa Pavlovich married the minister of agriculture, had twin daughters, and appeared on television as a news broadcaster. Soon afterwards, her wealthy husband, fifteen years her senior, died. She consoled herself by buying a Swiss chalet in St. Moritz. She liked mountain climbing and skiing.

Ambition propelled Laryssa quickly upward. She did not waste any time in achieving her goals. She wanted to integrate herself into the Belarusian political world. And she would use what she had to accomplish that: her beauty and her brains.

First, she became a broadcaster for Belarus's Russian-language television channel; then she was appointed director of television-media for the administration. And next, she became the press secretary, a position which she agreed to cultivate and expand.

She met an hour a day for breakfast with her team and the president to review the news of the day for the public. It was said that he conferred with her for his press releases and speeches, due to her knowledge and foresight in foreign affairs. Some say she became the ideologue and strategist of his policies. Her critics claimed that everything he said in public was written first by her. But I imagine that Laryssa intentionally kept her influence secret. She was smart enough to realize that in such a position she had enemies.

But Laryssa made a mistake. She laughed at a comedian who had phoned Lukashenko, pretending he was Putin. Lukashenko took the call, and she made fun of it. Laryssa was dismissed. Lukashenko had declared, "No one laughs at me!"

Laryssa then retired to the countryside. She claimed she was interested in living a quiet life in her farmhouse that she had received as a perk while working for Lukashenko. She wanted to educate her daughters.

For many years, she was called the "Red Iron Lady" of the Belarusian political horizon. After retiring from the ministry, she tried to keep her private life private. And there was nothing to hide. Her daughters were growing up in the countryside like many other Belarusian teenagers, and she was busy gardening and cooking and hosting parties.

Yet, the press would not stay away from her. Citizens were still intrigued. She was considered the most stylish woman in Belarus, although she was often attacked by local designers about her love for black and dressing like an American. The press became fixated on taking photos of her wearing glamorous jewelry and expensive clothes. They wondered if they were gifts. They refused to allow her to retreat from being the center of interest in their country.

I kept reading, mesmerized that this had been written about someone I knew. How was all this possible? She was so cerebral in front of my Zoom screen, so fixated on discussing film from her modest wooden table. I never suspected anything like this!

I clicked on another link, thinking I had made a mistake when Google gave me another surprise. The article read:

> UNITED STATES DEPARTMENT OF THE TREASURY SANCTIONS LIST AGAINST BELARUSIANS:
>
> Alexander Lukashenko, President of Belarus since 1994 has been actively criticized by the U.S., E.U., and U.N. for human rights violations during his presidency and fraudulent election results. Because of this, he has been sanctioned by the international community. In addition, various Belarusian officials, with links to the authoritarian regime of Lukashenko, have also been subjected to sanctions which involve asset freeze and travel bans. They are listed below in the U.S. Department of the Treasury Sanction List:
>
> Laryssa Pavlovich:
> ID: 3371072A012PB1
> Assistant to the President and former Deputy Head of the President's Administration. In her previous capacity, she was in charge of media, legal and justice issues in the President's Administration and was directly responsible for organizing the fraudulent elections in 2006 and 2010.

This was shocking to me. This was the type of thing I read in newspapers about strangers—not about someone I know!

I also started to worry. Why is she late? I looked around to see if anyone was following me. Or waiting for her. Anyone suspicious. I felt my stomach become queasy. My head began to throb with a headache. I felt my blood flow through my veins. My face felt hot. Should I be here?

Why am I so curious, I reprimanded myself. Am I playing with fire? Snooping on an enemy of my country? Why do I like her? How *can* I like her? Is she a person to trust?

This brilliant, beautiful woman had captured my interest. She had awakened the writer in me. Was this my once-in-a-lifetime opportunity to learn about a tyrant through someone who knew him? I had no choice but to use my positive relationship with her and observe her more closely—to learn more.

At that moment, I decided to take the risk: allow this woman to become my teacher—switch sides with her. I would spy on her.

First, I needed her to trust me. I had already started this without realizing it. The groundwork had been set. Two years ago, when she first became my teaching assistant, I shared with her my ancestry that three of my grandparents were born in Minsk and one in St. Petersburg. She was pleased. It seemed to mean a lot to her.

And as my classes continued, she continued to request to be my TA for four semesters—an indication that she liked and trusted me. In hindsight, the two years during COVID had been an ideal circumstance for my curiosity as I now started to plan to write a novel. My habit had been to come to the Zoom screen five minutes early, and so did she. We shared an interest in film and we both enjoyed the pleasure of chatting together before the class started.

I was the professor, even the scientist, putting her under a microscope, searching for traits to document.

And now, two years later, I was developing our friendship, reinforcing the stage for my spy thriller. Foreign Films were bringing us together—movies of politics, history and espionage.

As I continued to wait, I kept worrying. Why is she so late? Usually, she was extremely punctual for our Zoom classes, even early. Had she changed her mind about meeting me? Did she think our friendship was dangerous? For her? Or me?

Concerned that she might have been detained for a reason, I walked over to the security office, to check to see if anything suspicious was happening. I remembered her quivering voice over the phone. Perhaps she was in trouble?

I was worried that she had been followed. Had she run away to hide? I considered that my meeting could be dangerous for her. I didn't want anything to happen to her because of me. I started to blame myself for putting her in a compromising position. I wondered, should I be encouraging this friendship? Then I started to think of myself, objectively—my role in participating in dangerous politics, my link to a possible lethal outcome.

While searching for her, I peered into the security room filled with X-ray machines and saw myself in a two-way mirror. I stared at my image as if I were a character in a book. And thought, how would I describe myself if I were a protagonist?

At five foot five and narrowly built, my most distinctive characteristic are my eyes. Brown with a touch of gold when I'm happy or sad, they say what I sometimes cannot. Slanted, my eyes seem to be in balance with my high cheek bones, a trait from my Russian past. My nose is slightly wide because it had been broken when I was ten years old—due to my being a poor baseball catcher—and I never had it fixed.

My hair is chestnut-brown, very straight and fine, and worn to the nape of my neck. I always try to blow-dry it into the shape of a balloon, but it stubbornly refuses to comply, instead looking like it's flying on its own.

My weight has not changed since high school, and at 125 pounds, I continue to wear my comfy "vintage" clothes. I rationalize that I'm too busy to shop. Instead, I adorn myself with necklaces, a different one every day, and in doing so, I satisfy my taste for style with an international flare.

My age? That's a secret that I guard, and claim it's just a number. I reason that it's my soul that remains the same, ageless, despite years of challenges and obstacles.

I tend to be high-energy, and any challenging project attracts my spirit. Some say I'm feisty, others say indomitable. I say, I just can't give up. I love life too much. My earlier and terrifying bout with cancer had only heightened this determination. Coupled with this is a sense of humor that has saved me many times when things are heavy; when my shoulders are just too narrow for the weight.

CHAPTER 3

Bomb Scare at the United Nations; Films and Life: The Certainty of Chance; My Friend is Her Father's Daughter

---

As I was studying my image in the mirror, I saw and heard a UN guard running and yelling, "Leave the premises!" Frantically, he was screaming, "Everyone get out!"

He looked panic-stricken in his attempt to appear in control. He shooed me away with a group of others and pointed to the security gate while shouting, "Leave! Hurry!"

The lights went out. Darkness shrouded the entire complex. A siren blasted. I heard screams. What's going on? What had happened? Chaos. People scrambling to safety. Guards pointing to exits. I tried to pick up the smell of a bomb or a fire. Had an explosive detonated? Had there been a blast? I kept running.

"Evacuate!" the UN guards bellowed again, practically pushing people out the gates.

I saw a bomb-disposal unit comprised of a swarm of policemen, dozens of them running toward the building. They were dressed in gear I had never seen before—oxygen masks, helmets, protective clothing, carrying machine guns. Their heavy boots made the ground next to me vibrate as they stormed by.

I ran. Where should I go?

I looked around, other guards yelling, "Disperse! Get out!"

Women in saris, men in turbans, diplomats, tourists, children—all pushing frantically to leave the premises.

At the gate, more guards were yelling, "Get as far away as you can!"

I asked an elderly man navigating slowly what he thought had happened.

"A bomb. Terrorists! In the Security Council Chamber."

He sounded convincing. I helped him down the steps and led him to First Avenue.

"I'm going north," I told him.

"I'm going south," and he pointed towards 42nd Street.

Once I saw him manage on his own, I crossed the avenue and ran past the American Mission, a newly constructed building that had large holes sculpted into its façade. When it had been first built, I thought the design resembled Swiss cheese. But today, I realized the architect's intent: bullet holes across the street from the United Nations.

I rushed. I ran as fast as I could and went towards 47th Street and the Japanese Mission. There was a bench behind the Mission in a protective corner of their garden. I grabbed my place next to several others who had sought safety, like me. A man was seated nearby in a chair, talking nervously on his cell phone.

The Japanese clock rang strong. I tried to count the rings but couldn't concentrate. Often, from my classroom, I could hear the loud bells from the garden, and I'd pace the continuation of my lecture to its time. But now, the chime reminded me that you can't trust time, and that danger can happen when you expect it least.

Laryssa was still late, and if she arrived at the UN at this moment, she'd never find me. What would she do? Should I text her?

As I was considering what to do, a man next to me whispered, "All safe. I hear the clear signal. I've heard it before in Baghdad. But in New York? Who would have ever thought in the most guarded city."

I picked myself up, followed him back to the UN and returned to the scene of the crime.

"Must have been a false alarm," he reassured me. I did feel better, but still, a little shaken up.

I returned to the plaza, eyeing the iconic pistol twisted for its aim of peace, and looked around to survey if Laryssa had arrived. I decided to wait another few minutes and turned my thoughts away from danger to my film classes. It would calm me.

I remembered the film that I had just screened several weeks ago in September, *Faces Places*, directed by Agnès Varda. The New Wave director was coming full circle with her career as filmmaker and photographer. Her goal was to fuse the still (photography) with the moving image (cinema) to create a new way of filmmaking. As an artist who created her last movie at eighty-nine years old, she used chance to dictate the content of the film. "*La certitude du hazard*," she said. The certainty of chance. Not opposing poles, as one would think of the scientific versus the artistic, but joining, as it is in life.

She wanted to create a visual form of storytelling—unplanned, unconscious, with no rigid structure, no written text—just the chance of art to freely tell a story.

Her film emerged from the experience of a mature master, using history of cinema with life experience to give an art form for the people of villages while taking photos of their faces (*Faces Places*). She created for them a gift that would become her legacy of gratitude for allowing her to be an artist.

As I had lectured to the class about how Agnès Varda used and took advantage of chance and the unexpected to relinquish her control for art's sake, I was hoping to get a reaction or comment from my students, but they were listening, silently.

I had moved on to another topic. We talked about artistic creation, and how the *process* of creating is more important than the end result—that is, for the artist.

Laryssa shook her head and smiled. That was enough for me to realize that she was understanding, and that my TA and I were on the same side. I kept testing her, trying to learn more about how she thinks. I was hoping to discover a secret about her from her analysis of a film.

I didn't realize it then, but now as I look back, I was also learning from Laryssa about life. I remember how excited she was to share her thoughts with me.

"One of the most important themes in life," Laryssa commented, "is time. Agnès Varda wanted to bring the past to the present, for the future. Her vehicle was photography with cinema—to merge them as one in a new visual optic, a different way of telling a story. It's a little like what Proust did in literature."

"Yes!" I replied. "It's known that any of the five senses can wake up the past for the present. For a few seconds, this can happen due to an unconscious reaction. Proust used taste—the taste of little cakes, petites madeleines, that he used to eat as a child. Eating them again, later in life, became a vehicle for him to recreate his life when he was a child. Bring back the past to the present so memory would not die. He wanted the beautiful part of his youth to live on in his literature—in his art. He began writing the day his mother died. He didn't want to lose his past or his mother."

Laryssa understood. "I'm sure we all mix the past with the present, unconsciously or consciously. Like with smell—the smell of flowers—roses that can take us back for a few seconds to a special time in the past when we loved someone. . . We don't want to lose that love forever . . ."

She stopped talking and became emotional. It was so unlike her. I wondered if she was thinking of a lost love. . . Someone from her past that she kept secret in her memory. Someone special. She had given me a window into her character. Would I ever be able to find out about Laryssa's secret past?

I thought of the film that we had seen last week, *Persepolis*, written and directed by Iranian, Marjane Satrapi. Before the entire class had entered our Zoom, Laryssa told me, "I loved this film. It spoke to me because when I was three years old until I was eleven, my parents lived and worked in Beijing. My father was an ophthalmologist and worked for the medical division of the Russian embassy there. My mother had been a nurse and assisted him.

"From Beijing, they were reassigned to Tehran for two years. Both China and Iran would not allow young children to stay in their country, so I lived with my grandparents in St. Petersburg. My parents visited me very often, every month. When they were in Iran, it was during the Islamic Revolution when the Ayatollah had returned to Tehran from Paris."

While Laryssa was relating her story, I listened with my ears, but my mind kept spinning. I had to filter what I thought was the truth from what she was telling me, based on my studies of Russian espionage. It must have been the Russians who did not allow her to leave St. Petersburg. They kept the child in the motherland as collateral so her parents would not defect to the West. They must have been spies to have been given such a position in China, and especially in Iran, since Russia needed to spy on the new Islamic government—perhaps getting ready to solidify Soviet relations with Iran for the future. For today.

I thought of the many years it takes a country to solidify geo-political relationships, as with Iran and China. Russia has been a business partner with these two countries for decades. And during the Iranian Revolution, perhaps that relationship became stronger as their common enemy, the US, united them. Today, more than ever, Russia and Iran are tied together by the same common enemy. "The enemy of my enemy is my friend."

I wondered, what were these two partners, Iran and China, currently doing with Russia in the Ukrainian war? Iran is Russia's primary supplier of thousands of missiles and drones—Shahed exploding drones—that Russia uses to target Ukrainian power plants, electrical stations, hospitals, schools, homes, playgrounds, children, people in the streets . . . people just trying to live. Iran's missile arsenal is the largest in the Middle East and is a supplier for Russia in the Ukrainian war. The nuclear program for Iran and Russia is a ticking bomb. Russia is the world's biggest nuclear power. And Iran is their biggest provider.

These two pariah countries, Iran and Russia, are also uniting financially through their banking system to circumvent Western sanctions. Together, they have created a messaging service, allowing their banks to make international deposits and payments, even transactions in cryptocurrency. The system connects 700 Russian banks with Iran and thirteen other allied countries to form a massive network with hundreds of banks.

They live by the rule: economics precedes politics.

And then there were refurbished weapons that unite Iran and Russia. Weapons from retreating Ukrainians that are captured and seized by Russian soldiers and sent to Iran to reverse-engineer the systems. In many cases, these weapons are American and Western arms that are being dismantled, analyzed and refurbished and then recycled back to Russia.

I learned later through googling Laryssa again, that her father, once returning to St. Petersburg had been relocated to Minsk where he was made director of the most important ophthalmology clinic in Belarus. I presumed that this was his reward for service in China and Iran. Her mother was rewarded by becoming the director of a small theater in the capital.

And Laryssa had agreed with me as our class discussed that even under communism, there is no social equality. Some have more, some want more, and the privileged continue to get more. Her favorite English phrase was, "That's life."

I remember she told the class, "When I was nine years old, my father took me to our basement. He wanted to explain to me why he and my mother were living in China and then Iran. I was upset they hadn't taken me with them.

"Our basement had a secret room that was hidden behind a bookcase full of books. My father pressed a button, the bookcase slid into the wall, and before me, I saw a large room full of mysterious machines. My father showed me each machine, how it worked, and what its purpose was. He explained that he had to hide the machines in our basement because he used them to send secret codes to his superiors. No one was to know. I had to swear . . ." She stopped talking. I realized she stopped herself from saying that the secret codes were being sent to his superiors in Moscow.

Often, when Laryssa talked to the class, I had to reflect on whether what she said was a lie or a dramatic embellishment. It wasn't her heavily accented English that distracted me—it was her thoughts. When I had first met her, I wondered if her stories were true. They sounded so outlandish. It was only after time that I realized she was trying to explain to me, and to herself, what she had become: her father's daughter.

I looked at my watch, slightly annoyed, mostly worried. Where was she? Why so late? Should I wait?

My cell phone rang. Laryssa.

"Professor, I'll be there soon. So sorry. Please wait for me."

She hung up before I could reply. Of course I'd wait. I'd think of another film and try to uncover more clues about her.

Drive My Car, a Japanese Oscar-winner that used Chekhov's *Uncle Vanya* excited Laryssa. Proudly, she told the class, "There is no Russian writer greater than Chekhov. This week, I read *Uncle Vanya* again in Russian and in English. His Russian cannot be translated—it's poetry—he creates his own words and images."

She gave such a brilliant analysis, that I asked her if she had time for my next Zoom class with my undergraduate students, since I would be discussing the same film with them.

Delighted, she stayed on my Zoom class and began by telling these students, "My mother was the director of a theater. She believed that the 'Russian World,' *Russkiy Mir,* a concept advocated by Kremlin politicians, included 'Great Russia' (Soviet Republic), 'Little Russia' (Ukraine), and 'White Russia' (Belarus). She believed in a Russian imperialism known as *Ruscism.* A concept that promoted Russia's right to dominate neighboring nations. She predicted that the bordering countries would be united by the same Russian language, the same Orthodox church, the same government.

I listened and remembered that Putin had once said, "Where Russian soldiers walk, is Russian territory."

As she spoke, I sensed there was a conflict inside her. It was hard to decipher her true feelings. Was her mother right about Russia's future?

Mother Russia was politically and culturally for a return to the Russian Empire. Lukashenko had just ordered that all schoolbooks need to be written in the Russian language, not in Belarusian. Newspapers and TV would follow.

She told the students, "What I loved about my mother, who sadly is no longer with me, is at night, before I went to bed, she'd read to me the works of Chekhov.

"The character of Sonya in *Uncle Vanya* is, in reality, Chekhov. They both represent a spirit wanting freedom but symbolizing the opposite of unfulfilled ambition." She paused, sighed, and commented, "As a child, I'd fall asleep swearing I'd never be like Sonya."

CHAPTER 4

Who is the Real Spy?

The fog broke open to warm, sunny skies. I saw her; she came running, shouting an apology: "I had to do something for my husband at the mission. Professor, I'm so sorry," she apologized. "I had to send some attachments to Belarus for him. He only trusts me." Perhaps using machines like the ones in her father's basement, I thought.

At first, I didn't fully recognize her, accustomed to see only her face on my Zoom screen. She was much taller than I had thought, at about five foot eight. And she was thinner than I had imagined, yet surprisingly strong. Athletic.

Her face, as always, was intriguing, inviting, engaging. She had high cheek bones, sculpted below slanted eyes that were chiseled in deep blue. Her curly red hair was fuller than it appeared on screen. Like a majestic crown of curls swirling around her face. Full lips reflected the sun in a bright red hue that matched her nail polish. Her long fingers fluttered as she spoke like a bird freed from its cage.

Her entire persona was compelling. Despite her nervous apology, her body was straight and in control. She carried herself like a ballerina, with a long neck, elegant, and strength of self-confidence. As she rushed, she approached the square of the UN plaza like a force of nature.

Laryssa was dressed in American jeans ripped at the knees, wearing sandals as if she were strolling New York sidewalks on vacation. Large, dark sunglasses covered her face like a shield. She had a bouncy way of walking, as if dancing, free with all her body, and her strong presence didn't allow her to hide in any crowd. She attracted attention even though she tried not to. She had a different type of beauty: unorthodox but striking, reflecting a strong spirit. She was confident, indomitable. She stood out amidst the serious atmosphere of diplomats in the UN plaza. Everyone else was dressed in suits and dresses, going to meetings, trying to solve the problems of the world, while she gave the feeling of a free, liberated soul.

She was carrying a rectangle package wrapped in aluminum foil. It was about five by twelve inches, and solid like a brick. "Professor Edwards, for you . . ."

I interrupted her. "Please, we're friends, call me Sybil."

"Are you sure? I don't want to be disrespectful."

"If you don't call me by my name, Sybil, I'll be insulted."

She smiled and handed me a gift. "For you . . . Sybil . . . a loaf of cake I baked," she said, smiling, as she leaned forward to offer her respects and say hello.

"Giving cake in Russia and Belarus means offering friendship. My hobby is to bake cakes for my friends. I like to use raisins and nuts."

She opened the package in the center of the plaza for me to smell, as if we were at a party and not at the UN.

In a Proustian moment, I was taken back to my grandmother's kitchen in New York where Russian music played, and the air was warm with her baked cakes filled with my favorite golden raisins. I pictured my grandmother's round face, flushed and smiling, offering me apricot-filled blintzes, and thick beet Borscht. She'd kiss me on the cheek. "You must be hungry."

I told Laryssa that family circumstances caused me to live with my grandparents. Like her. Not in St. Petersburg but in New York.

"They spoke Russian at home," I told her. "My grandmother had been an opera singer and my grandfather a musician in the Czar's orchestra. The only time I saw a man cry was my grandfather when he watched a film on TV about how Rasputin was killed. He shared with me his precious memory of the monk who was often at the Czar's evening concerts.

"My grandfather often spoke of the Russian monk turned mystic. He said that Rasputin had told him how much he loved the way he played Russian Romani songs with his violin. My grandfather was so proud of the compliment.

"Cakes of all kinds," she explained, "are a symbol we offer to our friends when they move into a new house. Or start something new. It's meant to wish them good luck with something sweet."

My thoughts returned to the woman standing in front of me, and I noticed that her right thumb was bandaged. Why would that be? The bandage she wore was a strange type of gauze—not at all the type my husband kept in our bathroom cabinet. My concern for her grew.

"What happened?" I pointed to her thumb.

"Oh that," she waved her finger, flippantly as if it was nothing at all. "Banged my nail last week with a hammer when I was in Minsk. I was renovating my house in the countryside that I finally got back."

I wondered if her house had been sanctioned. And what had happened to her Swiss chalet?

"It's a farmhouse not far from the capital. A country spot, a little like your house in Connecticut that I see sometimes from your Zoom screen when you're there."

"Yes, a good place to run to—what we did when COVID was rampant in the city."

"Maybe I'll write a novel in my country house," she said. "Like you did."

"You'd have a lot to say."

"One would think so," and she gave me her cryptic smile. I smiled, too, thinking she'd be a great spy writer.

"And now, from New York, how often do you go back and forth to Minsk?" I asked her.

"One week once a month."

"Expensive commute," I commented.

"I need to see my daughters. And my father is in Minsk; he's elderly and not well. I have my housekeeper living with them."

"And then there's your farmhouse to oversee." I smiled, trying to engage her more, and yet, realizing I should ration my curiosity if I wanted to keep her confidence.

"Yes. I don't want to live any more in the city."

I found that curious—such a brilliant woman to forfeit the intellectual stimuli of urban life.

"Too much violence after the 2020 elections," she commented.

Ah-ha—I had her. "What do you mean?"

"My apartment overlooks the main street in Minsk called Communist Street, *Kamunistycnaja,* down the road from Victory Square. Lee Harvey Oswald, who shot President John Kennedy, lived in my building in 1959 for a few years with his Russian wife, Marina. I knew her well after she divorced. She's older than me, but an avid member of my chess club.

"I remember she had told me that she would have done anything before she met Oswald to leave Minsk. At the time, her comment meant nothing to me. Lots of people felt that way. But her marrying Oswald and leaving for Texas, carried a big price for her."

Laryssa shrugged her shoulders. I imagined she was thinking, "That's life."

She continued talking, "Oswald worked in Minsk at a radio and TV factory, Gorizont Electronics. His apartment was monitored constantly by the CIA from 1959 to 1963. They were investigating him to figure out why was he discharged from the American Marines; why did he want to live in Russia; why did he desperately try to return to Russia the September before Kennedy was assassinated; and ultimately, why did he kill President Kennedy in Dallas in 1963.

"Oswald was also being followed by the KGB, who suspected that he might be a spy for the CIA. They forced him to live in Minsk so it was easier to watch him than it would have been in Moscow. The espionage unit in Minsk was assigned to follow him; so, they surveilled him from an apartment next door, which was on the floor where I have an apartment now.

"At that time, the KGB redid the neighboring apartment and installed thin walls with a peephole and magnifying lens that opened secretly into Oswald's bedroom."

"Was he a spy?" I asked, half-surprised.

"Who knows? For the CIA or KGB? It's hard to say. And even harder to say who assassinated President Kennedy—if Oswald did it alone or if there was a conspiracy. And why would Oswald do it?

"But the KGB continued to be suspicious of him—why was he in Russia? They had his company transfer him to Minsk and placed him in my building which now has become well-known because of its location. It overlooks the main square where they've had riots after Lukashenko's 2020 election."

"What do you mean?"

She explained, "I was in my apartment the night of the fraudulent elections in August 2020. Legally, Lukashenko lost. The people didn't vote him in. More than thirty-five thousand demonstrators were arrested. Thousands more were beaten up and left bleeding in the streets. Lukashenko had his police make sure he remained Europe's longest living dictator.

"That night, it was like a horror movie. But it was real!

"The square filed up with groups of students, then workers, then thousands of people to protest a dictator they didn't want. They came united for freedom—for themselves and for the future of their children.

"The police came to stop them, beat them up. There were soldiers from the National Guard, the Army and KGB, all dressed in black leather coats, black helmets, black shields, looking like swarms of black beasts.

"Tractors, snowplows, garbage trucks, rolled into the square to run down the dissidents. 'Freedom! Dignity!' rebels screamed, yelling for their life.

"One after one, police and soldiers slammed iron poles into a body as if they were killing a fly. Thousands were left bleeding in the streets. Those fleeing were arrested.

"An old man was being beaten by the police. People watched as the man doubled over, blood was spilling out of his mouth. Powerless bystanders shouted, 'No more!' But the violence intensified. Hatred was mixed with savagery.

"There was no stopping the hysteria from the crowd."

Laryssa wiped tears from her cheeks. "I prefer the quiet of the countryside."

* * *

We decided not to have lunch at the UN, but nearby at a café on 44th Street. That had been my suggestion. I had remembered that they had just installed a new security system inside the UN building, located next to the dining room. I didn't want to go through a security check with Laryssa watching me. Sometimes, the alarm would ring as the metal prothesis of my arm appeared on screen, and a female guard would have to search me separately outside the room. All very embarrassing. Something I'd prefer to avoid.

I was also concerned that there might be another bomb scare, which I had not mentioned to Laryssa. But I subtly suggested that the sun was out and it was perfect to sit outside at the "Audrey Hepburn Sculpture Garden." It was a popular UN spot adjacent to the UNICEF building. She didn't know it and was curious. I was relieved that she agreed.

While we were seated, Laryssa was concerned that I kept moving my face away from the sun and offered to find another table in the shade. I was impressed with her caring.

The first thing she asked me, was, "Sybil, based on your reading, would you say the war in Ukraine is an example of genocide?"

I had to think quickly. Why was she asking me this question before any other, and how would I answer?

"Well, let's first define what genocide is."

After ten minutes of discussion, I concluded with, "Yes. Ukrainians are being attacked, killed, destroyed, and eliminated because they are Ukrainians. Why should this be?"

"Genocide is accompanied by war crimes," she commented in a voice that didn't sound like hers. Her chiseled face lost its strong shape.

I thought of a newspaper article the previous day in the *New York Times* stating that investigators in Bucharest, Romania, are starting to gather facts about Russian and Belarusian crimes against humanity. They had already collected thousands of pieces of proof for war crimes to be used at the Hague.

The strategy was to first gather evidence about the frightening numbers of Ukrainian children who've been abducted to Russia and forced to become Russian citizens. Boys and girls aged eight to eighteen are being trained as soldiers to fight against their fellow Ukrainians. Those up to eight are sent to orphanages, and infants are put up for adoption and sold.

Her leader has been facilitating many abductions with his personal vans.

Laryssa was quiet, so unlike her usual manner. She would typically chatter away in her accented English. But now, she was silent, thinking.

I took a deep breath and considered changing the topic. It was too difficult for me to absorb that investigators in Romania would identify Belarusians as well as Russians who are involved in kidnapping children. The thought of her even knowing about this horror, or involved in any type of war crime, was painful for me. I thought of her as my friend and didn't want anything to happen to her.

She was concerned about Russian and Belarusian officials being called to defend themselves at the International Criminal Court in The Hague. I realized she was worrying about herself.

I thought to comment but remained silent. I held back, not wanting to hurt her. Yet, I was fully aware that war criminals should and will be held accountable for their crimes, even if the accused are sentenced *in absentia*.

I was tempted to change our conversation to small talk. Genocide and crimes against humanity were upsetting thoughts to me. And I was sure that they were painful possibilities for her. But I refused to allow this to happen while continuing to chat with Laryssa. I realized that this was an opportunity to learn about her, as well as about her country. I wasn't ready to stop.

"Please tell me about your city, Minsk. I've travelled a lot in northern Europe, but never to Belarus."

Her expression remained motionless. She nodded her head, understanding that I wanted to change the conversation, but she continued to be pensive, because she knew the facts about the war. World War II in Belarus had not been good at all; in fact, it was little different from what's going on today in Ukraine.

"Because of bombings during World War II from Germany, as we were with the Allies and Russia, our country was destroyed," she commented. "Minsk was completely razed. After the war, our capital had to be rebuilt.

"It's very modern today," she explained. "We have a rich cultural life—sixteen museums, eleven theaters, 139 libraries, an opera house, several concert halls, and a metro system that displays art and photo exhibits underground.

"Dining out is special. Most restaurants have musicians who entertain with a wide range of music from Romani songs to jazz to classical. We even have comics performing and actors reciting poetry."

She stopped, smiled, and added, "Lots of chess clubs, each one with interiors decorated in a different style—some of modern glass, some of antique stone. And there's always a special room for a cybercafé located on the lowest floor.

"Chess and books are our national treasure," she added, proud of both.

Yet oddly, I remarked there was a strange faraway look that came to her face. Unusual, because she usually had an intense expression, and was very focused. I never knew if the serious look was because she struggled speaking English or she was controlling each word she was saying. But now her look seemed dreamy.

"Do you play chess?" I asked.

"Yes. Chess is very important in Belarus. Each city has dozens of chess clubs. Minsk has almost one hundred. All the clubs are very busy and it's exciting to enter a club, although it's extremely quiet inside. Chess in Belarus is considered an art with practice, practice, practice.

"Emphasis is on rigorous training and study of the game, especially the moves and strategy. We have many important masters in my country."

"Are you a master?"

She didn't answer, only gave me her enigmatic smile.

"I've played chess since I was five years old. At ten, I was a member of the National Junior Team. We'd go to championships as a group to other countries like Poland, Finland, Estonia."

"Did you ever win a tournament?" I was thinking of my son, a two-time fencing Olympian, winning several world cups.

"A few, some junior championships."

I smiled trying to imitate her cryptic style and nodded my head in understanding. She was modest, as well as reserved, and would never brag about winning. It was only later that I realized how important chess and chess clubs were to her—her secret activities. And how active she was with chess. How it was essential.

But at this moment during our lunch, chess was just a topic for light conversation. I sensed she didn't want to talk any more about it, and I thought it was best to return to our discussion of Minsk, a subject that seemed to relax her.

"What do you miss most about your city?" I asked, trying to return to neutral ground.

"The café life, my friends I liked to meet. When I was a student, we had our favorite bistro where we'd go after dinner. There was a piano inside . . ." She paused, remembering. A shadow of darkness covered her face. "I would sing. My friend would play the piano for me . . ."

I decided to change the conversation again. Her faraway expression looked haunting to me. An escape wrapped in memories.

I held my breath and tried to recall what I had learned in my world history class in college: 52% of the population of Minsk before the war was Jewish. There were one hundred synagogues throughout the city until the German occupation destroyed them all. Most of the Jews were killed in their country or sent to Sobibor concentration camp to be exterminated.

Hundreds of thousands of Orthodox Christians were also forced to march to labor camps as slave laborers. Thousands of villages and towns were burned and destroyed; millions of Belarusians were starved to death as the Germans plundered the entire country.

More than half the population of Minsk was either killed or forcibly displaced during World War II. Nothing like this could be said of any other European city. About 1,200,000 houses were turned to ashes. Minsk lost over 80% of their buildings and city infrastructure.

I didn't bring up any of these facts that I had remembered. And chess and bistros were topics to return to . . . but not for now.

CHAPTER 5

A Death in Minsk—What Does it Mean? Checkmate in Chess

On the Wednesday after Thanksgiving, we had our Zoom meeting, for which Laryssa and I came a few minutes earlier than other members in our class.

I asked her how she was, and she gave her standard cheerful reply, "Just fine . . ." She then elaborated on how she felt things had gone. "I celebrated two Thanksgivings. One last Thursday for our American friends, in which I prepared everything myself: turkey, cranberries, stuffing, yams, pumpkin pie, and Russian desserts."

"Wow!" I was impressed.

And she continued. "The next day, Friday, I prepared even more for eleven of us at the Mission. Even our men got involved by decorating the dining room."

I remembered that the Mission of Belarus was located near Lexington Avenue in the 60s, set behind a tall, wired fence with multiple cameras. All members of the Mission lived there in private apartments. The basement was digitally equipped for video transmissions and spyware.

"Thanksgiving two times," I commented. "You must be tired."

"Well . . . yes and no, not actually tired . . . but a little . . ." she hesitated, searching for the English word. And then she said, "distressed."

"Why?"

Her previous cheerful face turned somber. Strained.

"Well, our foreign minister was found dead on Saturday in Minsk. He was rather young, and in excellent health." I saw her take a deep breath, close her eyes.

"No one knows how . . . He was my best friend since our university days together."

"Oh, I'm so sorry . . ." I didn't know what else to say. Each week, I read about someone from Russia who fell out of a window (pushed), or drank tea spiked with chemicals (poisoned), or was in a car or plane that had an accident (exploded) . . .

Until that point I had never thought of someone I knew being poisoned. Poison that kills. Poison without an antidote. I wondered what she was thinking.

If the foreign minister was her best friend, they must have shared common thoughts. Was she afraid that she could be poisoned next? Who would poison her? The Belarusians? Russians? Ukrainians? Was I endangering her by meeting her? I was the American, an enemy. I wondered if I was I endangering myself. Maybe I should see her only on our Zooms, and not meet her for coffee or lunch. This could get dangerous. Poison is not a joke.

The more I thought about it, the more frightened I became for her. Was she playing Russian roulette? Did she like this high-risk game? Lukashenko had just signed a law that any official or army member convicted of treason would be executed within twenty-four hours. One bullet in the head. No one dared play Russian roulette with him.

"Oh, that's terrible," was all I could say.

She nodded her head, looked down and remained silent. She covered her eyes with her hands. She was obviously very affected.

I didn't know what to say. I felt nauseous, filled with worry and fear. For her. For me. This was not a child's game of cops and robbers, spies and tyrants. I told myself to stop.

After several minutes, she looked up at the screen, took a deep breath, and said in a fairly cold manner, "That's life."

A chill went through me.

There was another long silence. I know she had been distressed by her friend's death, but her refrain and comment, were too controlled, too icy. Was she an actress? What was she revealing to me? I couldn't be sure. Should I attribute such clues to her many-sided character?

I was overwhelmed by what she had just told me and how she had reacted by saying so calmly, "That's life."

I wondered if this habitual phrase of hers was her way of accepting what she couldn't control. It's possible that underneath her hard skin, she was afraid. I couldn't stop sensing that she was playing a game of high risk.

Not knowing how to respond or what to say, I was hoping that another student would enter our chat room. But she and I were still early, and we remained alone.

She, more in control than me, spoke first.

"I enjoyed very much our film for today, *Tar*," she commented in the same controlled voice. "Cate Blanchette is amazing . . ." Laryssa paused, searching for her next English words. "I guess you can say it's a film about power."

"Yes," I agreed. "Power. Tar asks, 'What does power look like, feel like, not only within an institution but within an individual psyche?'

"She's a figure who cultivates power through her arrogance," I summarized. "She uses her power over others and abuses it." I wanted my words to sound like a warning, but Laryssa didn't hear me. She was lost in her own thoughts.

"Power," she whispered, "is the result of ambition."

"What do you mean?" I asked her. Our role of professor and student was changing again.

"The highest reward of ambition is to have power over people. One achieves it from money or politics." She hesitated and added, "Ambition becomes an obsession. Once you taste a little of it, you want more. Ambition is a drug, an addiction. When you have it, you get the highest high."

She gave a cryptic smile. "What could be better than to achieve control over people?"

I thought she had spent too much time with her guru Lukashenko and his Russian buddies. Autocrats. Greed. Wanting more money, more territory, more control. Was she joining them—driven by the same obsession to have more?

Laryssa appeared to still be in her own thoughts. She made a movement with her hands as if she were dismissing my thoughts of caution.

"Abuse of power," Laryssa commented. "That's Tar's crime. But also, the abuse of the rules. She gets emotionally involved. Emotions can't be part of rules. One has to do what one has to do. And one has to know what is right and wrong. In total control. Without emotions!"

Laryssa struck her fist on the table where her computer's screen was placed. She raised her voice and repeated her words—"Without emotion!"

I had the feeling she was speaking from experience—about something very important that had happened to her—about a time when she had to act without emotion. To choose the rules. I wondered if it was about a love in her life. A man? And now she was remembering. Perhaps she was trying to rationalize what she had done. What she had chosen—the rules, not the man. She clearly had her secrets.

Laryssa continued talking. "There is something I can't understand—why did the screen writer use Russian names? Lydia and Olga are the most common female Slavic names. And Krista is the feminine for Khristos—Christ in Russian. Is the movie saying something about Russia?"

Wow, I thought. I hadn't noticed that in the film. But she had!

"Well," I answered, trying to remain the professor. "Who is the most powerful person today in politics? Putin. And like Lydia Tar—a bully. He has destroyed millions and millions of people." As I spoke, I became more and more angry. "He's the symbol of power that destroys! Power that turns evil!"

She looked at me with a shocked expression. I had lost control. We both paused. I took a deep breath and waited for my anger to pass.

Still, I wasn't up to answer any more questions after hearing about her friend's death and her comment, "That's life."

I remembered seeing his picture on when I had searched for her picture on Google. They were laughing together in the photo, and now he was dead. I was rattled. I tried to regain my restraint. I hoped I would have the strength to lecture for two hours and talk about a film—with Russian-named characters—as she had just reminded me.

I tried to stop thinking how her friend had died—was he one of those who had been eliminated for not agreeing with the government? Poisoned?

Their photo kept appearing in my mind. They seemed so happy together. The text under their image had said that Laryssa Pavlovich was confident and ambitious, and was often at the center of political scandals. But—the caption pointed out—one person whom she never criticized was Foreign Minister Vladimir Makei.

I had clicked a link to learn more about him. Vladimir Makei had been trusted ally of Lukashenko since 2012, and is known to be a bridge for the Belarusian government, linking the West with his country. He is a pro-Western sympathizer, and he has represented his country in meetings with the US, the UK, the UN, and the EU for a decade. An adviser to the Ukrainian Minister of the Interior had even said that Makei is one of the few people in Belarusian politics who is not under Russian influence.

As I thought about him, I wondered, was it good or bad for him not to be under Russian influence? He was trying to move his country toward the West. And she was his friend. Was she trying to do the same? In her own way?

To use her influence—her power—to bring a dictatorship to a democracy? Was that her ambition?

"What do you think, Sybil?" she said, interrupting my thoughts. "What's your opinion about power in personal relations?" She was clearly eager to discuss the film. Or was it power that she wanted to analyze?

I wondered if watching movies had become her escape from reality. Had I given her that outlet? Did we both share the same refuge? Art usurping life, because life was too difficult to face?

"I've been with my husband for several years," she told me.

I was always eager to hear her speak about her private life, but now, I found it sacrilegious. Yet, she continued. "We've been together since he was assigned from the military to become attaché at the United Nations. In the beginning, I commuted to Minsk for my work for two years. But it became too complicated, especially at customs in New York. When I'd enter the US, I'd be questioned, sometimes searched, taken to a small room."

I wondered if she had problems because of international sanctions. She was on the US Department of Treasury sanction list. I had seen that on Google. Was she using a diplomatic passport as the spouse of the military attaché at the United Nations to make entering the US easier?

I knew from friends that such a passport is a *passe partout.* It gets someone in and out of any country. A diplomatic passport can be used instead of a personal passport—even if someone is on a sanctions list.

I didn't say anything. She continued, talking. I was thinking of her golden passport, and why she needed it. Was having it part of her plan? Her ambition? Clues . . . I was trying to piece together the character on my screen.

"So, I chose to stop working in Minsk," she commented, "and instead, help my husband in New York. Like his silent partner. Since I've been working with him, his career has gone up." She indicated the ascent with her hand, moving her red manicured fingers up to the ceiling. "And I have become more useful in doing so. More noticeable to my government."

I wondered if she has ambitions that he'd become the next foreign minister. Or did she have such ambitions for herself? There were several European countries who had female prime ministers as well as presidents. What was in her mind?

Could she be involved in a change of government in Belarus? Or was her ambition to have total control over people—like an autocrat? She obviously thought she could. Her ego was limitless. So was her ambition.

I was scared for her. She was playing a high-risk game. I remembered a Chinese proverb, "A bird that flies too high is shot down."

I tried to tell myself that my suspicions were simply my imagination. The writer in me was trying to spin fiction with facts. What comes first, life or art? Reality or fantasy? Do they ever intersect?

I tried to stop thinking—it was making me very nervous. I glanced at my screen to see if there was a student who had entered the class. Bingo! Someone did! I told Laryssa that we should save our talk for another time.

She nodded, always polite. I wondered, if her proper manner was just a mask—her cover-up like makeup for an actress.

Laryssa quickly gave me an indication of what she really thought by ending the conversation with the comment, "I can't wait to discuss with our students if they think Tar will be punished."

And then she said as she lowered her voice, "I wonder if political autocrats all over the world will be punished!"

It was then that I realized that underneath her bravado, she was afraid.

As I absorbed what she had just said, there was a part of me that felt sorry for her. I liked her. I was intrigued by all the conflicting sides of her character, as well as all of her opportunities to do what's right—in her own way.

I truly wanted to be her friend.

* * *

After our Zoom class finished, and everyone left the chat room, Laryssa asked me if I had time to go out for coffee. She wanted to get some air. I felt the same way and realized she must be upset about the death of her friend, the foreign minister.

"Sure, what about we meet at our favorite spot?"

Café d'Oro was midway between our residences, within walking distance for both of us. I enjoyed going there; it made me feel I was at a café in Europe while still being in New York.

I walked to the restaurant, practically in my neighborhood. It gave me the opportunity to think. Somehow, I always thought more acutely while walking, as if the movement of my legs stimulated the movement of my brain.

I couldn't help but wonder: Why does Laryssa like me? Is it to keep her job as TA? Is it to learn from me, a professor? Or is there something else—maybe something transactional, or manipulative? I didn't want to get overly suspicious, but I wondered: if there were a tribunal for crimes against humanity, how would I feel?

I hoped nothing would happen to her. And I hoped she wouldn't ask me to vouch for her—to appear before a trial and jury as a witness for her good character.

She has become to me more than just a student. I felt sorry for her conflicts. I understood her difficult situation and saw the good and the bad in her. My maternal side wanted to help her.

Thirty minutes later, we arrived at the same time at the café's swivel doors.

She looked tense, dressed in black, not wearing makeup. Her curly red hair appeared static, as if our city wind had attacked it and blown her crown to a frizz. We took the first table available and gave our order for espressos. Her cell phone rang. She stood up, walked to the corner of the room, speaking in Ukrainian or Russian. I didn't know the difference. I studied the menu. She quickly returned, apologized, and tried to smile.

Beginning the conversation, she asked me, "Have you ever watched a chess tournament?"

Chess was obviously important enough for her to revisit the subject from our last conversation. "No," I confessed. "Maybe a couple of times on TV, but never up close. Certainly, not like you. I guess you've won a lot of matches."

She didn't answer. Instead, she stared at me, looking at me directly into my eyes. Then she turned her body very slowly several degrees to the left and then to the right. She dropped her scarf, picked it up and turned around in her chair. She looked like a ballet dancer doing subtle moves. But I realized she was looking to see who our neighbors were. She stood up, turned around once and sat down, quietly. Then she pulled her chair closer to me. I sensed she needed to talk.

Moving her chair closer to the table, she leaned over to me and whispered, "I believe you want to learn more about me." It was more a statement than a question. I wasn't sure if it was an accusation. How did she know? Was I so transparent? Most likely, I'm not as good as an actress as she is.

"I have a great deal of respect for you and maybe, one day I will need your help. . . Yes, I believe I will." She paused, staring hard at me.

I felt a chill pass through me.

"A secret of mine today for your loyalty for the future," she stated, like an ultimatum for our friendship. It sounded like a deal. "Do you agree?"

"Sure," I said, clearing my throat.

"For this loyalty, I am going to share with you a side of my life that I know you've been wanting to see." She gave me her elegant hand to shake on our promise, which I did. I noticed her manicured fingers fluttered with confidence.

I suddenly felt guilty. Snooping, prying—it was not the way to treat a friend. And now she was offering me a reward of information. She had realized what I had been doing. And she forgave me. I felt emotional, like a kid getting caught while glancing through a friend's diary.

I nodded my head and said, "Yes, you have my loyalty."

Laryssa whispered, "Let me share something important with you."

She stared at me, hard. "Promise never to tell."

"I swear." I raised my hand and kept my unmanicured fingers steady.

She began.

CHAPTER 6

Chess in Minsk: Masters and Spies; Secret Truths

"I told you that chess is very important in Belarus. The emphasis is on training and study of the game—choices of moves and strategy. But for me, chess has become a way to free myself from guilt."

I stared at her. Often, she spoke like a Sphinx.

"Chess is known among grandmasters to be a psychological warfare. In order to win, you must break down your opponent's ego."

It was a little like she, the Sphinx, was speaking another language to me. And it was taking me time to understand.

"During this war with Ukraine, I am using chess as a tool for practical warfare—a means to an end."

Slowly, I began to understand her, especially when she said "Military war is also psychological—to slowly break down the enemy's ego. To win, you have to overcome the adversary by finding an opening of weakness, then striking!"

I stared at her. She was comparing the basics of war to chess.

"In war, as in chess, there must be a strategy with specifically planned sequences of moves. The leader of a country moves his soldiers like his chess pieces."

I listened—she was the political strategist, professor, and chessmaster.

She continued to explain: "I have used my connections at multiple chess clubs in and around Minsk. My connections are with members of an anti-Russian underground movement in my country."

I tried not to react to her words. I remained quiet hoping she'd tell me more.

"I started my campaign in Minsk. I knew someone personally in each chess club in the capital and I knew for sure that the person was anti-Russian. Many people in Belarus have family that lives in Ukraine. We can't go against family." She took a deep breath and then, slowly, continued.

"In each chess club, I designated one anti-Russian player to be my contact and to be in charge of identifying for me which other members of the club are anti-Russian and willing to join our group.

"I work with my sister-in-law, Alina, who lives in Kyiv. Guided by Alina, who's allied with the Ukrainian army although she is Belarusian, I've organized my chess players into a grassroots underground movement. We are known as 'Isola Territorial Defense Force.' Our mission is to identify and destroy Russian spies who have been sent to Belarus by the Russian government. And there are thousands of them who've infiltrated our country.

"How does this work?" she asked me.

I shrugged my shoulders and moved closer. She was now in charge. We were changing roles.

"The chess players use their cell phones to take secret videos of any Russian in the streets of Minsk and in other Belarusian cities and towns. We can identify them by their clothes—Russian fabric is coarse, and Russian boots are not made of leather, but a type of rubber that looks like leather. They typically walk two by two, speaking loudly, often drunk, looking confused about where to go. The signs of our streets are written in Belarusian. They can't read them.

"Once our chess players have taken videos of them, they code them with navigational coordinates which they find on Google Earth. They send the codes and passwords to specific Ukrainian soldiers who work in the middle of the night inside Belarus, secretly, and who go to the location to look for the enemy during the day and then again, at dark.

"Each night, dozens of Russian spies are killed by Ukrainian soldiers; the numbers are now in the hundreds. Members of our underground movement comprised of the Belarusian chess players are part of a special cyber section of the Ukrainian army. They have created a sense of fear that pervades the cities and towns of Belarus like a plague.

"Why? The chess players are masters. They are also spies, using their talents to detect transmissions from cell phones that belong to Russian soldiers who are also spies. But in this game of espionage, the Belarusians are more motivated to win. They are facing the loss of their country.

"It is after nightfall that the Russian soldiers phone home. Their phone usage allows the Belarusian chess players to detect the signals and zero in on their location. Each cell phone message from the enemy becomes a transmitter, a stationary target to pinpoint a hiding place. And then our members attack.

"Our chess masters claim, 'I never knew that I loved my country so much that I would kill a person.'

"The last time I was in Minsk, I went to multiple clubs to talk to my partisans. All of them asked me the same question and gave me the same answer: 'Why am I part of this Resistance?' They told me, 'The Russian spy wants to destroy my life, my family, my friends. I can't bring back those who've been killed. But I can render justice with revenge.'"

Laryssa stopped talking, her face was becoming flushed. She took a deep breath and continued.

"Chess players, old and young, become a link in a chain to expose Russians who aren't legally documented or allowed to be in Belarus.

"The chess masters do not use guns, only their cell phones. The Ukrainian soldiers are the ones with ammunition. The chess players become their underground soldiers, cyber war agents. Once known as nerds, these chess players set up a special Morse code telegram system that they're able to use at their chess clubs. Other members might think they're researching chess moves, but in reality, they're searching for enemies.

"The chess players are so well organized that the Ukrainian army depends on them as an auxiliary patrol.

"Last week, they located a hotel where a group of Russian spies were spending the night, using the hotel as their base. The Ukrainians set fire to the hotel.

"Do you want to hear more?" she asked me with a slight smile on her face.

"Of course," I said, leaning closer to her.

"Our chess masters found another way to detect Russian soldiers at night." She paused, grinned again and continued. "The Russian soldiers have big coats and blankets."

"What do you mean?" I asked.

"At night, they cover themselves from the cold. But the blankets and coats are too short and their long arms, legs, and head stick out. Instead of concealing themselves, their body heat gives them away because the Russian blankets create cold spots against their body heat. The Ukrainian drones use special night vision sensors and thermal imaging that detect these contrasting bodily cold spots." Then she started to laugh in such a strange way that I got scared. "Ironically," she said, "the Russian soldiers lead the Ukrainian drones to them like sitting ducks."

Laryssa stopped talking. Her high cheek bones were the color of her curly hair, appearing like red bombs on fire. Her blue eyes were wide with adrenalin. The skin of her face looked tight. Her body was rigid and controlled. I, the American, felt like a baby in a lion's den. War. She was talking about real war, with bombs, killings. Spies and secrets. Underground resistance fighters. Computer nerds in disguise to save their lives and country. She was sharing with me some very private information, information that I wasn't sure I wanted to know.

I tried to imitate her control, *sang-froid,* as the French called it. Cold blood. Something I realized she conjured up when she needed it. But it was hard for me to do the same.

I wanted to ask her if she thought that Putin was a champion chess master. A grandmaster KGB agent making his moves on a chess board that was the entire Baltic region. Each country was his goal to conquer—to get back his empire. He was making one move at a time. And he, the king, the grandmaster, would win. But I dared not ask.

While I was listening, I realized that I had sworn loyalty to her—her, the *chess master*—and I might one day have to pay her back for her secrets. Help her—I had now promised to. And I would do so if I could. So, I believed, because of my future debt, I had a certain number of rights in our relationship. I wanted to remain the writer, the secret spy without saying outright that I was writing her story. For this reason, I needed more information.

First, I wanted to know more about Lukashenko, her supposed boss. I dared not ask what his game was. He probably knew little about chess and was not aware of her members and their chess moves or spyware. I'd be happy just to learn some details about him that I could use in my book.

As a woman, I was curious to know if Laryssa had had an affair with him. I couldn't escape my female curiosity. News articles on the internet never spoke openly about a love affair, but they did comment on the fact that they were always together when she worked in the ministry. The photos did show a form of intimacy when they chatted, as she leaned into him to better hear his comments, always appearing to be smiling. She had probably learned in Sibiu how to command her body to satisfy any man.

She had been married once, before she worked for him. Her husband had been many years her senior. But then he passed away and left her with two small children. She was morally free to return to work with the dictator. . . And . . .

She was presently married for the second time. Theoretically, not free. But now, still working closely with the dictator, did she resume their intimacy? My feminine side was so intrigued . . .

Still, I couldn't ask her how close they were. It's too personal to talk about a relationship with a man. My curiosity did have limits. Although, I was tempted as a writer to know more. Spy stories and love affairs go together.

Instead, I began by asking, "What is Lukashenko like? You must know him well."

She nodded her head. I could see her thinking how to be careful in describing him or what she'd tell me. Perhaps she thought I was wearing wires to a tape recorder. Or her being circumspect was the mark of a true spy. I could never be a spy. I talk too much.

"He's clever, with a strong survival sense."

Obviously, I thought, to have existed as a dictator for three decades. But I didn't comment. Like her, I tried to measure my words. And I wondered, was she aware of my cat and mouse game.

"He has a terrible temper." She raised her hands to let her fluttering fingers speak for her. "He fired me because I laughed at him during a press conference. A journalist had asked him, 'Why did you get angry when one of our comedians called you on the phone and pretended he was Putin, and you fell for it?'"

"Wow!"

She shrugged her shoulders. "He rehired me a few weeks later. Claimed he needed me to quiet down his journalists."

I laughed and nodded. Women all over the world love to use their power. "I guess he wanted to forgive you." She gave a quick nod and furtive smile.

Then she added, "His new law is that anyone who's convicted of being a pedophile, will be chemically castrated."

"Oh my God!" I dared not ask what chemically castrated meant in her country. I knew what it meant in my country.

Instead, I asked her, "What's he like as a person?" I was determined to learn more about her personal relationship with the dictator.

She navigated my question. "He likes to wear English custom-made suits, French ties, Italian shirts, and American shoes. Makes him feel like a citizen of the world."

"What else about him?" I was becoming more and more curious.

"Well . . . he's strongly built. Very muscular . . ."

She should know, I thought.

"That's because when he was a teenager, he was a pig farmer. Not much money in that. I think that's why he never wanted to be poor again. All his choices, private and political, have been based on how much money he can stash away. Today, he's the second richest politician in the world after Putin."

She paused, flashed her red nails in a dismissive manner.

"Not only is he strong, but he's athletic. Often on Sundays, he'd practice with our national hockey team."

"I heard you have a good team," I commented.

"Yes," she nodded her head. "We've won World Cups and European championships." Then she added, "Lukashenko was interviewed after a hockey practice about his stamina. He replied that 'it's better to die standing than to live on your knees.'"

I laughed. I wondered if she still had feelings for him. They still work close together. It's always hard to give up friendships—especially with a powerful friend.

She hesitated to say more. I saw her thinking. She acted as if she were avoiding a pothole while driving a car. Probably, she thought the less said is better than more. But then she lowered her head and said in a soft voice, "I used to be minister of sports."

"Wow!" That impressed me. And she was being modest about it.

"The trouble with our young athletes," she said, "is that we support them and then when they start winning tournaments, they leave our country. We lose them.

"I had previously invested a lot of money sponsoring our girls' tennis team. I even paid for summer training camps in Spain. Once they reached the top ten, they were recruited. I never saw them again except on TV."

She picked up her cup of coffee, put it down and started laughing. I smiled at the unexpected surge of levity.

"What's so funny?" I asked her.

"Lukashenko. He said the most ridiculous thing during COVID. Our country was really affected. The only vaccine that was available was the Russian Sputnik." She laughed again. This time with a scornful tinge.

"He went on TV and said, 'COVID here? In our country? I don't see any flies or insects flying around. The best treatment is to ride a tractor, visit a sauna, and drink some vodka afterwards.'"

We both laughed—two friends enjoying some fun.

"He claimed that's the best remedy. He dismissed the coronavirus as a mass psychosis. The fault of the Americans. But he's also a hypochondriac. He's Europe's longest dictator and wants to stay the last living dictator."

I could understand that. He has a lot to lose.

"He's afraid of being poisoned . . . or . . ." she hesitated to finish her words. "He's lost consciousness several times. Odd, it's always at a meeting with Putin."

"Stress," my husband always said, "could kill us."

"They say he has a blood clot condition. But who knows?" She shrugged her shoulders. "Basically, he's not too smart," she concluded. "He has zero foresight. He sold his soul to the devil—for money. His philosophy has always been: there must be more."

Then she paused and whispered, "He doesn't realize he's sitting in a trap by being Putin's puppet. The people despise Lukashenko because of that. They've been planning a coup d'état for years. He tries to bolster the economy to quiet them down, but for that he needs contacts from the boss. And the people hate him even more."

She paused again, then looked up, starring hard at the ceiling as if she wanted God to hear her. "Power and money have a price."

A chill went through me. I'd had the same feeling when she told me about the foreign minister's death—a death most likely caused by poison.

"That's life," she whispered to finish her description of her dictator.

I remained quiet. I was unnerved. I attempted to change the conversation, say something, but I saw her thinking. I was also thinking also that it's hard to tell where her allegiance is.

Her cell phone rang again. She stood up, went to the corner of the room, spoke in her language, a little longer this time, a little more emotional, a little more bitter. Then she returned to the table, and now in control, apologized.

"That was my husband. I probably should return to the Mission. He may need me."

"No problem," I said. "I have a doctor's appointment."

She looked at me with concern. I was touched but gave no explanation. I saw her eyes glance towards my arm. Silently, we both stood up.

She took her coat and made a slight attempt to pay for her coffee.

I protested. She kissed both my cheeks goodbye and fled through the swivel doors.

CHAPTER 7

A City of Surprises; Pity and Pleasure

Despite good health for thirty years, my husband insisted that I continue to get a yearly checkup to assure my blood counts were normal.

The routine was familiar—I'd go to the hospital where Carmen, the technician in the oncology department, would give me a blood test.

She'd take my index finger, cut the skin lightly with a special needle, and allow several drops of blood to fall on a glass slide. Then she'd insert the slide into a machine while I sat and waited, always nervously, until she'd see a green light blink and a digital sign indicating that all was well. Then the slide with the blood sample would pop out. She'd give me a thumbs up and I'd give her a hug.

While waiting for a printout of the blood count, I'd rub the puffy scar extending from my elbow to shoulder. Hidden under my skin was a cadaver bone set in place with titanium bolts and rods that never bothered me unless I had to pass through a security system. The scar reminded me of how much I should appreciate life—and I did. I had looked at that scar every morning and every evening for thirty years. I would never forget how lucky I was.

Next, was an X-ray to assure that the cadaver bone was firmly intact. This time, the radiologist I knew was not there. His substitute, a young resident, didn't read my chart, and instead, asked me questions: "How long have you had your prothesis? What's the diagnosis?"

"Angio-sarcoma of the right humerus."

"Wow!" he responded. "And you're still alive! Is that really the diagnosis?"

"Yes."

Embarrassed, he turned off the X-ray machine, and whispered, "Good luck." I dressed quickly, left the hospital building while taking deep breaths. Then I rushed outside to be part of the living.

* * *

New York City was quiet after New Year's. Many residents were away; snow bunnies who could had escaped to warm up from our historic frigid weather. I kept thinking of the poor people of Ukraine, without electricity or heat. How they were forced to set up living quarters and schools in subway stations to avoid bombings and cold. How could we in the US complain about a few days of discomfort?

I had received a New Years' greeting from Laryssa and answered by asking her if she had time, would she like to spend the afternoon exploring some new neighborhoods in the city. I offered myself as her guide. We decided to meet at noon for a coffee at Shakespeare & Co. near her Mission.

As usual, I arrived a few minutes early. Nearing the bookstore, I saw Laryssa on the other side of the avenue. She was walking with a man, who was several inches shorter than her, many years older, and wearing an overcoat that was frayed at the sleeves and collar. It was too large for him and gave him a frail look. His face was pale and taut, with thin lips and a small nose that was shadowed by wired eyeglasses. His beard was gray and pointy, in the style of Lenin. He wore a Russian-style fur hat that was too large for his small head and slipped down his forehead as he walked and talked.

Could this man possibly be Laryssa's husband, or was he simply a colleague?

When they parted, he gave her a mechanical nod of his head, and she did the same. How odd, I thought. My husband, Gene, in a similar situation, would give me a big smile and a kiss on the cheek.

The man left her, slipping into a shadowed street corner to go his own way. Laryssa saw me watching, waved nonchalantly, and ran across the street to greet me. "My husband was in a rush; otherwise, I would have introduced you."

"No problem," I said with the same nonchalance. "I hope another time to make his acquaintance."

Continuing in my controlled manner, while walking to the 2nd Avenue bus, I showed her an old paper map I had of the city, suggesting some interesting spots we might visit. She quickly agreed. Neither of us commented about her husband. Instead, we chatted about how Manhattan is a city comprised of neighborhoods. First on our list was Alphabet City.

We rode the bus southbound as we chatted about New York City, both of us realizing that this was a subterfuge to avoid talking of a piercing, painful war. Each month, another million Ukrainians were leaving their country. The end of human suffering was nowhere in sight.

After thirty minutes, I commented, "Alphabet City is our next stop. Are you hungry?"

I suggested a café I knew on the corner of Avenue C and 6th Street, The St. Barth, a trendy French café where they serve crêpes and homemade soups. Perfect for a January day.

The St. Barth is a popular spot for NYU students who live in neighboring dorms in Soho and south of 14th Street. As soon as we entered, we felt the warmth of the fireplace and the burning logs. We walked over to the red flames as if they were magnets, offering us their warmth. All the walls were of red brick splashed with a fine layer of white paint giving a feeling of old New York. The ceilings were high, made of tin in the original style. The floors were of wooden parquets, softened with multiple area rugs of different sizes and colors. There was a sweet fragrance from evergreens that made me feel as if I was in the middle of a winter garden.

Every table was a display of young, happy people, all dressed in their own creative fashion, drinking lattes and homemade *glühwein* to warm their conversation. There was a buzz in the room, and I enjoyed taking it all in.

We stayed a while and then continued on our journey through the city to mid-point at the East River and Sutton Place. This was a section as old as Alphabet City, but unlike its southern sister, it was groomed and chiseled for the privileged few. Historic townhouses blended in with private gardens hidden by stone walls, high gates, bushes and trees. Periodically, at alternate streets, there were openings, allowing one to view the East River as a reminder that the city was built on an island.

We walked over to another of my favorite spots to admire the 59th Street bridge. Recognizing the short promenade on Sutton Place, we entered the square to enjoy the sight of a group of young children on scooters and toddlers attempting to run despite their heavy wrappings. Their sweet faces emerged from scarves and coats as if they were Santa's little elves not caring about the winter cold.

Mothers and nannies picked up little ones who had fallen and repositioned them to start again. It appeared to be an oasis of goodness where neighborhood children were free to play in their own world, unknown to adults outside the square.

We lingered awhile, leaning against the handrail, swaying toward the sun reflected at the river's edge. We admired the buildings of steel shimmering in the light while listening to the laughter of children nearby. There was a goodness in the air, a music of toddlers at play. I listened to become a part of it and lingered a while.

"How about one more New York site before the evening sets in?" I asked, reluctant to end our day.

Her cryptic smile gave a quick reply, "Yes. I'm enjoying this so much."

We took the York Avenue bus to 96th Street and then strolled over to Fifth Avenue.

On Park Avenue, we crossed at the light despite its warning not to. Suddenly, a long, black car raced in front of Laryssa. She was busy chatting. I was listening, but as was my habit, I was also eyeing the bicycle path. While surveying the lane, I saw the black limo aim at us. I jumped to the side and pulled Laryssa away with my left arm. It was an awkward movement from me because my right arm was next to her as we walked. Habit had made me unable to use my right arm—especially to pull someone away from danger.

The car zoomed onto 95th Street and the driver yelled something from his opened window. It sounded to me like threats in a foreign language.

"What was that?!" she cried, losing her usual calm.

"A car aiming at us."

She took a deep breath and paused a few seconds. I thought I heard her speak some curse words in Russian. I remembered that whenever my grandfather cursed, it was in Russian.

She had clearly understood the driver's warning, but—not wishing to share it with me—she said: "Must have been a drunken driver."

I accepted her response to be polite, although I doubted its veracity, and kept my eyes focused on the road. Sometimes Laryssa lets down her guard and a movement of her eyes or emotion on her face can reveal what she's really thinking. Anger. Fear. I sensed this was one of those moments. I wondered if the car had been following her. Whose side were they on? Does she know too much? Did someone want to eliminate her?

When all else fails, I try to change the conversation by using some benign small talk. This was the right occasion. "I still have some cake you sent me for Christmas that's in my freezer. I'm saving it."

"I'm glad I was able to give you a little pleasure."

"Do you cook other things?" I was trying hard to forget that we had just been a target. Of whom, I was afraid to ask. But I felt that Laryssa knew.

"My favorite dish for holidays is a Russian dish my grandmother taught me: *Pelmeni*—small dumplings served with grated onions, cheese and potatoes."

I wanted to forget about our narrow escape, so I kept chatting "Please tell me more about your country."

About that subject, I was truly interested, since it reminded me of times with my grandparents. I also thought she needed to calm down a little more, too.

"Yes, let's talk," she understood my motive without questioning. "The official religion of Belarus is Orthodox. But recently, with the war, there's a new division of faith in our churches. For centuries, the Belarusian Orthodox church was under the Russian Orthodox church that has its center in Moscow and is pro-Putin. But since the war, there has been a split in Belarus—a major change. Many Belarusian priests have turned against Russia.

She continued, "Russian soldiers dressed as priests are hiding in churches throughout Belarus. They use the church as a place to collect millions of dollars. Then they buy guns and hand them out from the church basement. They're spies! And only the rightful priests know who they are.

"Even our UN Mission, with eleven members living and working on the upper East side, is full of spies! I'm sure they're spying on me every day. And I have to smile to them." She sighed and bit her lip.

I felt so bad for her. I could sense the many conflicts she dealt with, as well as her need to survive and surpass this war. Living in a communist country had hardened her skin. I saw her rub a gold charm on a chain that was around her neck.

"What about you?" I asked. "Do you go to church at home?"

"I'm a believer in humanity—in peace. If the leaders around the world had a son who'd be drafted, they'd change their opinion about war. I don't like war. I wish I could do more against it."

We crossed to Fifth Avenue, taking the sunny side of the street parallel to Central Park. I thought the side near the park would be safer, that it would protect us from any other "drunk" drivers. And I felt that I needed some sun.

At 96th Street, we eyed the path northward and climbed up a hill that led to a dirt path marked for cyclists. Both of us felt relieved to be in Central Park when it was empty of people.

As we hiked, I played my tape recorder and listened to music. After ten minutes, we approached an opening at Fifth Avenue and 105th Street and walked toward the gate that was cast in a style of Old Europe. The sign said "Conservatory Garden," and entering, we walked toward a large rectangular lawn that was strangely still green in the winter.

On the right was a hidden trail that led to another circular garden with a fountain in the center that was capped by a metal sculpture of three dancing maidens. The water spray had been turned off to protect the pipes from freezing.

We walked into the next section, admired the shapely circular bushes. In the middle was a tall Christmas tree decorated with colored balls made of wood. Tinsel paper covered the green tree in an array of holiday cheer. It was beautiful and we lingered to absorb the symbol of peace.

As Laryssa was taking in the calmness of the scene, her eyes focused on a bush where she saw a woman leaning against the branches. It looked as if the woman was trying to protect herself from the wind. She was very still, like a frozen statue wrapped in a ragged coat and frayed scarf.

Laryssa walked over to her, moving toward the woman's backpack that was decorated with a Belarusian flag.

As the two of them talked in their language, the woman appeared to wake up from her frozen stance. She seemed animated by Laryssa's soft words. They talked for several minutes as I looked on from behind some tall bushes.

I studied the scene—both Laryssa's body movements and the woman's reactions. Laryssa's frame looked soft, not her usual rigid stance. She took out her purse, emptied the coins and all of her dollars into the woman's bare hands. Then Laryssa took off her woolen scarf and leather fur-lined gloves and handed them to the old woman.

I saw the woman try to kiss Laryssa's hands, but my friend pulled them away. She touched the woman's cheeks, and then both of them wiped away tears.

Slowly, Laryssa turned toward me and said, "Let's go. I have my bus card. That's all I need."

As we waited for the bus, Laryssa whispered something. I didn't know if she meant it to be for me or for herself. I heard the faint words, "I had to prove to myself that I'm not all bad."

CHAPTER 8

Secrets and Clues—What they Mean; Survival—More Important than Love

We walked toward Fifth Avenue in silence, leaving the secret garden behind us. I wondered if I should turn to see what the old lady was doing. Was she staying, leaving? Where would she go? Laryssa didn't say a word. Instead, she wiped more tears from her cheeks.

And then, overcome by emotion, she asked me, "How would you define crimes against humanity? Could someone hide from an investigation? Go to a country where there's no extradition? Like Mexico?"

Was she thinking of how Trotsky tried to hide from Stalin? I remembered Trotsky was killed despite the fact he was hiding abroad in the house of his communist friends, Frieda Kahlo and Diego Rivera.

I did not know the answer. I only sensed her passion to survive; I looked at her with compassion and gave an apologetic half-smile.

We continued walking, each one absorbed in their own thoughts. I spoke first. Long silences always made me feel uncomfortable. In addition, meeting the old woman had upset me. And I felt sorry for Laryssa's very obvious suffering.

I decided to ask her a question unrelated to anything we had ever discussed before and perhaps, learn more from her.

"If you could have a miracle come true, what would you wish for?"

Laryssa stopped walking and stared at me as if she were wondering if she could trust me with her innermost thoughts. Instead of answering my question, she said, "You first. Let me have some time to think."

I nodded yes and answered, "I'd want to see that each person around the world could work. That they could receive an education of their choice, which would allow them to be trained for a job they wanted. In this way, they'd be responsible for their work and be responsible to create their own life. They'd be free. Hopefully, happier.

"I remember I once got lost when I was on the subway. I was reading a book, and I missed my stop to get off. By the time I realized my error, I saw the sign 125th Street. Quickly I got out of the subway, feeling disoriented.

"I wanted to take the subway again and return home. But I had to go outside to cross the street to get the southbound train. It was raining. I didn't have an umbrella. Yet, despite the fact that I was soaking wet, I didn't run into the subway. I looked around to observe my surroundings. It was like I was seeing a foreign city. Sleeping on a cardboard box, I saw a man rolled up into a ragged coat. Despite the rain, he didn't move.

"I had twenty dollars in my wallet and placed the bill under his arm, hoping he'd find it. Then I walked a few streets until I saw a policeman and told him, 'There's a homeless man who's soaking wet on the corner at Lexington Avenue. Please help him get to a hospital.'

"What more could I do?"

Laryssa stared at me, also moved by the story, but didn't respond.

"The incident left me very sad," I told her. "That's when I thought if he had work, maybe he'd feel responsible to keep his job, and he wouldn't be out there, laying in the street."

Laryssa didn't answer. Instead, I continued speaking.

"That's my wish. A miracle. Maybe that's why I teach. To encourage people to think. To give them hope for a better life. People need to learn a trade or vocation or skill. And hopefully, that would lead them to a job and satisfying life."

Laryssa nodded her head. "That's a good miracle."

"Aren't all miracles good?"

"Yes, especially if they come true."

I laughed. "What would be a miracle for you?"

She hesitated, then said softly, "My miracle is less noble than yours. Mine is selfish." She cleared her throat as if she needed to make her wish more concrete. "My miracle would be to find the person I love."

She took a deep breath.

It was my turn to stare at her as I wondered, what does she mean? She obviously doesn't love her husband. I could only nod sympathetically, not wanting to pressure her for an explanation.

* * *

"Are you tired?" Laryssa asked me as we left Central Park for Fifth Avenue. "Would you rather take the bus?"

"No, not at all."

"Are you cold?" She was concerned as she watched me put on my gloves.

"No. Do you want mine?" I remembered she had given her gloves to the old woman.

"I'm fine." And she began to talk.

"I don't know if you noticed the old lady's eyes?"

"No," I confessed. I wondered where Laryssa's thoughts were going.

"Her eyes were the same color as my mother's—blue with a touch of green. My mother would wear green dresses and sweaters to bring out the green . . ."

She hesitated and then continued, smiling. "What I admired about my mother was that she was a free spirit."

"I guess you inherited that from her."

Laryssa laughed—something she didn't do often. Perhaps she was trusting me, opening up. We were becoming good friends. And I appreciated it.

"I remember my mother told me about an incident she had in Tehran. My mother and father were stationed there in the Russian Embassy. Belarus and Russia shared the same quarters.

"My mother had recalled that the incident was the price of being a free spirit. She refused to wear a hijab to cover her neck and shoulders, or headscarf to cover her hair, or veil to mask her face. And she refused to dress like an Iranian woman, in black, all covered up. She preferred jeans. She had a rebellious spirit that my father respected, but this trait was not always admired in Iran.

"My mother's greatest pleasure was to walk in a new city early in the morning and discover it before the city woke up. One day, as she was walking and exploring, and not wearing a headscarf or hijab, a group of teenaged boys began following her. She had natural blond hair that she wore long and full, curly like mine. And she never wore a hat.

"The boys followed her, calling out to her. She didn't understand their Farci, but she understood their interest. She tried to lose them by entering one store after another, but when she came out into the street, there they were, waiting for her, following her, taunting her.

"One day they threw stones at her. A policeman saw them and stopped them. But he blamed my mother and took her to the police station, accusing her of starting a riot. The chief of the Morality Police called my father at work, at the clinic in the Russian Embassy. My father arrived at the police station with the Russian Ambassador."

"Wow! What happened?" I was amazed.

"They got her out. The Russian Ambassador had contacts. And he had a weakness for my mother. He liked the way she looked in tight jeans." Laryssa smiled.

"A woman before her time," I commented.

"Yes, quite a role model."

We continued walking on Fifth Avenue; Laryssa was in a talkative mood. "You once told me that your husband was Romanian."

I noticed her speech pattern was becoming more natural when we chatted together, less accented as if she were not thinking while speaking. The words seemed to come from her heart rather than her mind. She was relaxing. We were interacting like old friends.

"Is he from Bucharest?" she asked. "Did he escape?"

"No, he left legally with his parents despite the communist regime."

"Really?"

"His father was a physician. Among his patients was an important government official, a minister. His father had his office in a separate wing of their house. The minister had admired the finely decorated home. He offered him a trade: three visas—for his wife, son, and himself to Paris where they had family. In exchange, the minister would take their house with everything inside it, including their art."

"Did they have a Brancusi?"

"No. But they had a valuable collection of Meissen porcelain."

"Your husband's family got the better deal—freedom."

I smiled. "And I got the best deal of all—my husband."

We both laughed. There was now an easy flow between us as we spoke. She understood what my husband had gone through to have lived in a communist country and then to find freedom. And yet, he had to give up his country, his language and friends—for freedom, yes, but also for the unknown.

I wondered if she envied him. Would she want to do the same? Her father, too, was a physician. And he had facilitated opportunities for her. He had been a spy . . . working for the Russians.

She continued. "I was in Bucharest when I was eighteen . . ." She paused, didn't say another word for a minute. She just kept walking, even increased her pace. She was athletic, with a strong stride and accustomed to the wind and cold.

Why and how did she get to Bucharest from Minsk? Had it been before Lukashenko's regime?

She interrupted my thoughts. "Did your husband ever return to Romania? Take you to visit Bucharest?"

Why was she so curious? It was not like her. Usually, she was hesitant to ask me personal questions as if she didn't want to give me the chance to ask her something private in return. Was she asking me now to pry open my secret world?

"Yes, we went to Bucharest in 1990, after Ceausescu was executed. Communism was over."

"That's when I went to Romania also," she said. "In Belarus, the controls were not rigid then. The window was slightly opened from 1989 to 1992, but then slammed shut in '94 when Lukashenko came in. He locked the country, herded us like cattle behind an iron curtain."

I felt her get sad. I liked her and didn't want to upset her. I changed the subject, something I realized I was doing often with her.

"Did you visit any other cities in Romania when you were there?" I asked.

"Yes, Sibiu, in Transylvania."

What had she been doing in Sibiu? How odd. And after 1989?

"I went to Sibiu for a few months," she said. "I was studying journalism . . . I went to write an article about Romania's agriculture . . ."

She stopped talking, abruptly. I realized she didn't want me to ask why Sibiu and why agriculture. Again, I was suspicious of her words.

I knew Sibiu. My husband had shown me the city where he had spent his summers as a boy. I remember how fascinated I was by the houses in the main square. "The eyes of Sibiu," they called the oddly shaped half-windows below the roofs. Built from the twelfth to fifteenth centuries by German-Saxons, the slanted windows offered air without allowing sun to enter the attic where they had stored cheese and grain.

Today, tourists discuss whether or not the slanted-eyed-shaped windows look like "Big Brother" surveilling the town. Many Romanians believe in the evil eye, which happens when someone is envious of a person and wishes evil. They claim that a curse in Sibiu is launched from attics behind those Slavic, slanted windows.

I marvelled—how appropriate for Laryssa to have spent time in Sibiu. Did it foreshadow Big Brother watching her? Did it shape her Slavic life?

"The previous leader of Romania," I commented, "President Klaus Iohannis, comes from Sibiu. He was the mayor there for nine years before becoming President. Iohannis is pro-Western and very close to the Americans. I heard that the CIA has its main operations for Eastern Europe in Sibiu."

Her body stiffened. Communication can go beyond words. I understood her reaction when I said CIA. Dare I ask what was she actually writing about in Sibiu? Certainly not agriculture—there's not much farming land in Sibiu. But her demeanor had warned me: no more questions.

Instead, I kept chatting just to keep the conversation going. "How did you find the people from Sibiu?" I asked.

"Friendly. Hard working, serious. Like their president, Iohannis."

I was hoping she'd give me some secrets from her life. Details that I could transfer to my literary character. Soft touches of truth.

"I met him a couple of times while I was in Sibiu," she said, casually. "We chatted in English, which is a safe language. Hard to tell where the other person comes from."

Yes, I thought, but how and why did she meet the President of Romania? And a couple of times, at that.

"I spoke English so his colleagues wouldn't know where I was from. People don't trust someone from Belarus or Russia," she said. "They think we're spies." She laughed. I felt a current go through my body like an electric shock.

"I was born in a prison," she commented in a strange tone. "Belarus is a jail. I learned at an early age that I had to survive—not tangibly; I had what I needed. My father was a doctor. But spiritually, morally—to be myself—to preserve my morals. I tried hard not to become a beast."

She stopped talking, picked up her pace of walking as if she had to rely on her strength and will power to control her words. She feared she was talking too much. A red line she had put in front of her, a limit not to cross.

It was an awkward rupture of conversation. I didn't know what to say. She had made her confession to me without giving me an explanation.

I felt like a hostage to her pain. Our lives had been so different, but yet, we came together in suffering. Secretly, I had also felt the despair to survive cancer. The fear of its return. Another type of hell. A prison that had left me handicapped. Her prison was political. Mine had been medical. And I, too, did not want to lose my ego. I refused to turn into a beast. Instead, I tried hard to become more understanding. And now, I realized, I was directing my empathy towards her.

Was there a connection to her being in Sibiu and her need to survive? What was her secret? She didn't say another word.

The wind picked up—New York's chilling wind—and I was feeling cold.

"How about if we take the bus?" I asked. "There's one approaching us."

"Good idea."

I felt she shared with me a relief to have closure to our walk and talk. Once inside the bus, she took out her cell phone, informed me that her husband had called her. She excused herself to return his call and walked to the rear of the bus. She had now regained her life as the wife of the military attaché of the United Nations. She had put back the wall between us. And I wondered: was this her way to survive? Is survival more important to her than love? Or ambition? What rules was she following?

Her chatter with me seemed to move in circles with little stops and interruptions. Her sporadic confessions contained many secrets. Potholes from life. The writer in me was trying to fill the holes.

This woman was a mystery. I watched her from the corner of my eye as she chatted with her husband in Russian or Belarusian on her phone. She appeared lost in their conversation. Was that her way to survive? Follow the rules of a game—to get what she wanted.

CHAPTER 9

Venom and Poisons; Crimes and Punishment; Plans to Visit Mexico

---

Several days passed. I was preparing to take my students from the UN and the university to a briefing at the Colombian Mission. I often invited my students to visit the UN or a Foreign Mission. This semester, the assistant to the ambassador of Colombia, who was a former student of mine, arranged for my classes to have a private briefing at her Mission. Beforehand, we saw the film, *Wild Colombia Revealed,* which is a photographic documentary showing the beauty of Colombia's biodiversity, and at the same time, a warning about the effects of climate change.

I began preparing my UN class for the briefing by asking my students about the Amazon. "Who knows something about the region?"

Laryssa, as always, despite the fact that she was not formally one of my registered students, was the first to raise her hand.

"The Amazon River is important for the region's water supply," she stated.

"Yes, of course," I agreed. "Water is needed for their abundant plant life. Does anyone know anything about plants in the Amazon and their relationship to medicine?"

Laryssa's hand was again first and this time, the only one.

"Pharmaceutical companies use important plants from the Amazon for their medicines," she responded.

"Yes. What plants?"

"Well, there's digitalis and aloe," she answered. "They're used positively, but there are some plants, even animals, that are used negatively. There are poisonous ones, like toad venom."

I was startled for a second. She obviously had poison on her mind. I wondered, if she was thinking of her friend, the foreign minister, who a Ukrainian official claimed had not been poisoned by Novichok but by toad venom.

"What's toad venom?" I blurted out without thinking. And then, I was afraid I had embarrassed her. Toad venom was a topic circulating daily about Russia and their deadly poisons. Of course she was concerned.

Laryssa grimaced. Her face appeared before me on the screen, and it didn't look like her.

I stopped myself from asking any other questions about plants or animals, especially poisonous ones. I was afraid that the responsible student in her would answer my questions and compromise herself without realizing it. I wanted to be careful of my power as a professor and curtail myself from going beyond limits of questioning.

"It kills." Laryssa blurted out before I could stop her. From the screen, I saw her face turn dark. I felt terrible asking these questions. I had to control my curiosity. She was my student, my friend.

I was fully aware then of how dangerous venoms and poisons of all kinds could be in eliminating adversaries. They had been used against so many: secreted into their food and onto their clothes. In the case of the Romanian dictator, Gheorghiu-Dej, a poisonous substance had been used on his bathroom doorknob in order to eliminate him. Each day, as he went to the bathroom, he'd touch his doorknob.

And I was sure Laryssa knew even more than me about such situations.

"Thank you for your answer, Laryssa," was all I could say. "Let's continue our discussion of plants and discuss how they reflect climate change."

I tried to move away from my screen, move away from myself. Correct myself and promise to fulfill my commitment to my students. My responsibility was to teach, to help.

Then Laryssa's cell phone rang. She stood up, left her computer screen, left her room, disappeared. Had I lost her? Perhaps she'd had enough of my prying.

I looked at my clock, wondering if she'd return. I was concerned that I had hurt her feelings. Was she aware of what I was doing? Spying?

Another student asked a question. "What about discussing deforestation in the Amazons?"

"Yes. Great topic."

I looked again at my clock. I was feeling guilty. Three minutes had passed. Laryssa returned. Our student from Norway talked about the Arctic and how deforestation and climate were affecting her country. A safe subject, I thought, and I allowed the Norwegian student's line of thinking to change our direction.

At the end of our two-hour class, Laryssa lingered on the screen, as was her habit. This time to reconfirm our luncheon date in a few days.

Feeling guilty about my probing, I said softly and sincerely, "How are you, Laryssa?" I truly liked her, and at that moment, I liked myself a good deal less. I was becoming too inquisitive. I knew I had no right to do so.

But she forgave me. She shrugged her shoulders, and she responded, "Everything's ok . . . I hope."

"I hope so, too. If you ever need me, remember, I'm there for you. I mean it."

"Thanks . . . I may have to take you up on that one day."

"You can count on me."

Her cryptic smile returned, and I felt pardoned, but still ashamed.

"So, we meet at noon on Monday?" she confirmed.

"Yes, at Café d'Oro."

"They still have their Christmas jewelry displayed for sale."

"I read that they're showing emeralds from Colombia."

We both laughed. Two women with similar tastes.

CHAPTER 10

Talk of Mexico

Winter in New York is frigid, long, and debilitating. Despite the month of Christmas decorations, which brighten the short days, New Yorkers grumble about the city's horrible climate. We share the common complaint about what is to blame: the wind.

Some neighborhoods of the city have more wind than others, depending on which skyscrapers have monopolized the sky and cause the wind to circle the streets. Whatever, however, whyever, New York's wind is cruel. Sometimes, it's so strong that one has trouble walking. It's a good thing that I'm often anchored down by weighty packages. In fact, most New Yorkers are.

I've found that the best antidote is a hot espresso, or a good hot meal, and a warm conversation with a friend. But perhaps best of all, is an escape to a sunny place.

I tried to give my attention to my hot pasta in my favorite cafe, eating it quickly so it wouldn't turn cold, while listening to Laryssa's chatter.

We talked of winter and holiday plans. I said my husband and I were planning to visit my brother who had just bought a house in Mexico.

She asked, "Where?"

"Near Cancun. An hour south toward Tulum."

"What a coincidence . . . I too, hope to go to Cancun, if we can get away. We have a business meeting next week, but maybe after that. I know some Belarusians who are living in Mexico. We've been there before, and I love it."

"Come visit us," I quickly said, ignoring her business excuse. "My brother has a driver who can fetch you. I can arrange for you to have him for the day."

"I'm not sure . . . who knows what tomorrow will bring?"

I saw her look down. Her face was obscured in dark shadows; her narrow shoulders slumped from their usual height. She looked smaller, shorter, frailer, older. I felt concern for her.

"Laryssa, you must remember that there is good in bad. Think that today you're living history; that's the good. You have secrets inside you. You're privy to your country's plans and future. And with secrets come opportunities. Good ones. They can become yours. Grab what's good!"

I saw her smile sincerely for the first time.

We continued to chat and moved to the more comfortable topic of film. Then her cell phone rang again. She stood up, walked to a corner, turned her back. I asked the waiter for the check and waved goodbye to her after I placed a few five-dollar bills on the table.

I looked at my watch, moved toward the counter with pastries, and waited my turn to buy some tarts and cookies. Some friends were coming for dinner. I smiled, thinking only of that.

CHAPTER 11

The Chinese Connection; More Mysteries

At our next film class on Zoom, I came early to the chat room as did Laryssa. I noticed that she looked tired. There were slight gray rings under her eyes that were highlighted on my screen that focused on her face. She looked worried beneath her chiseled façade.

I was tempted to ask her how she was, but she spoke first. "I'm going to Minsk next week. I'm not sure if I'll be able to Zoom into our class." She hesitated. "I might miss the film that I find the most amazing of all—*Jojo Rabbit*. Can you record the class discussion? And maybe we can chat about it when I return."

"Of course," I quickly replied. But what I wanted to ask her was why she was going to Minsk?

She must have read my mind. "I'm going to Minsk to see my twin daughters. Their 25th birthday is next Monday."

"How wonderful," and I smiled, truly relieved she had a happy reason. But as always, I wondered if that was the whole truth. Was she going to Minsk and then on to somewhere else? Maybe to Beijing?

I had just read in the *New York Times* that Lukashenko was planning to visit Beijing on Monday and was going to receive a red-carpet treatment and state reception.

The article had said, "Beijing opposes the meddling of international countries in Belarus's domestic affairs and sanctions on Belarus."

Beijing and Belarus have had business relations for many years. In 2022, there had been a 30% increase in trade for Belarus. And for the future, Belarus needs Beijing's business more than ever. If Russia should weaken, they'd have China as a backup.

I wondered if Laryssa's business trips to Washington involved her meeting with the Chinese. Or even meeting them in New York. It's known that Minsk is using Chinese parts to make rocket launchers and drones. Are the arms for the Russian war against Ukraine, with Belarus as the intermediary? Rumors even speak of nuclear weapons.

I wondered if her husband, the general, was involved in this. Was that their business? I remembered that her father had spent time working in China. Foreign relations take years to establish.

She had spoken often of her father's influence on her. Probably, he had paved the way for his brilliant daughter, his only child. Had he introduced her to his Chinese contacts?

I kept wondering whether she was actually going to China. Was such a trip a subterfuge on her behalf? Who was she spying for? The Americans would use her to get details about China's role in war and trade. And the Russians would need to verify the progress of such roles.

Baltic politics, Real Politik, espionage, and secrets.

I remember her telling me that China had built a special industrial eco-city twenty-five kilometers outside Minsk. It's a high-tech hub for 140 companies from fifteen countries, all centered around Chinese technology to be exported through Europe and Asia. This "Great Stone Industrial Park" is the world's fastest growing free zone of trade.

China can't work directly with Russia, so Belarus has become their substitute country for commerce. If China and Russia split in the future, China wants to have its feet in Europe and Asia. Belarus' location is perfect for such trade.

I remember Laryssa has asked me to show a film about China. "I'm starting to read about this country," she had commented. I wondered if and how she was involved in all this. Did she think it's more practical to get another Boss rather than Russia?

* * *

Laryssa returned to New York and eagerly wanted to meet. I was even more willing, and not just to talk about film. I wanted to know if she had visited China.

There we were, at our favorite cafe, sipping espresso, and I had China on my mind.

I began, "China has been very much in the news while you were away."

"Yes?" She didn't seem to be interested.

"Yes, China. American drones have detected that the Chinese are setting up eavesdropping stations in Cuba to spy on American space programs in Florida."

Laryssa didn't say anything. I had predicted she wouldn't comment.

"Have you ever been to China? I remember you told me your parents were working there while you lived with your grandparents."

"That's true. No, I've never been to China, but I remember my mother telling me something about a difficult situation in Beijing when she was at a cocktail party. It was held at the Russian Embassy."

She smiled, remembering.

"There was a high Chinese official who had a little too much to drink. He started to flirt with my mother, who diplomatically avoided him. She knew how to handle drunken men. Russians can get that way.

"In any event, he persisted. He asked my mother to become his mistress. Everyone in the room heard the proposition.

"My father came over to protect my mother. The Chinese official persisted with his request. So, my father had no choice."

"What did he do?" I interrupted her.

"He threw his glass of wine at the man, took my mother's hand, and left the party with her."

"Did your father get in trouble?"

"No, the Russian Ambassador intervened again. He had a weakness for my mother. The Chinese official got in trouble."

"Justice rendered," I said, and smiled.

Laryssa smiled, also. And then went on to another topic of conversation.

"I loved the film *JoJo Rabbit.* After seeing that movie, I knew I had to return to Minsk to see my daughters."

I listened, curious.

"Children, no matter what age, have to be protected. The father of my twins had died when they were young, not even teenagers. So, I had a responsibility to be the parent in charge. Growing up in a communist country is not easy for children..." She faltered as she spoke. I knew from my husband's past how difficult it is to live under a communist regime, especially for children who naturally love freedom.

"Propaganda is a tool that autocrats use going back to Hitler, as the film shows, to mold and destroy a child's mind. I hate such behavior!" she struck her fist on the table.

I jumped at the vibration, slightly embarrassed when our East Side neighbors at nearby tables turned to stare at us.

I couldn't help but whisper, "I agree." My reply sounded feeble to my ears in contrast to her statement based on her real experiences. Often, I wondered who the professor was. Who the spy? Our roles were intermingling.

"Yes," I said and nodded. "My husband was brought up under Fascism and Communism. He's still tormented by the hell he lived through."

Then I said, "Tell me about your daughters."

"They live in my old apartment with my father and a housekeeper who I've had since they were infants. Tanya is finishing law school and Clara is writing her dissertation in engineering. She's interested in cyber security."

I smiled, thinking she surely had an influence on their studies. "Do you have any photos of them? If you don't mind?

"Of course." She was pleased that I was interested. She opened up her phone to a photo of two beautiful young ladies with the same fiery red hair as their mother. Twins for sure, but not identical. One had shorter hair and brown eyes; the other one with fiery blue eyes and long hair. One looked extroverted and happy, the other more serious, like her mother.

"I heard a terrible thing while home in Minsk," Laryssa commented. "My daughters were asking me about something horrific they had heard on a vlog."

"What's a *vlog*?"

"It comes from Finland. A combination of video and blog with audio. Something like a podcast or YouTube, but private. You have to register and be approved. Each listener and participant must be first scrutinized. The vlog gives updates on undocumented legal cases from all over Europe.

"I watched how my daughters listen to their vlogs. They go into the bathroom with their radio and computer. Then they turn the water on in the bathtub and sink while blasting the radio. In this way, when they listen to the vlog from their computer, no one can hear it. We never know if someone is spying."

"What a horrible way to live."

"Children in Belarus learn at an early age how to survive. Unfortunately, they become hardened. After my daughters finish their podcast, they erase it." She paused, took a deep breath.

"This vlog was about the kidnapping of Ukrainian children to Russia and Belarus. Some of the children had been in orphanages or clinics or hiding alone in their destroyed homes in Ukraine. As many as 200,000 Ukrainian children have been taken by force by the Russian government. More than two thousand children, from one month to fifteen years old, have been transferred to Belarus. Lukashenko, himself, has signed the orders."

As she was talking her face was becoming as red as her hair. Flushed with anger, she continued.

"Each child kidnapped is registered. Their names are changed, as well as dates and places of birth. All this data is replaced by Russian names and ID. This makes the chances of their families finding them in the future very difficult, especially for infants and toddlers."

"That is appalling!" I was aghast.

"The children younger than five years old are put up for adoption. Sold like furniture in an auction. Boys and girls aged eight to eighteen are trained as soldiers to fight in the Russian army and kill fellow Ukrainians—their own people."

I listened, stunned. "Child soldiers. Kidnapped. No one is stopping them?"

"Russian authorities shrug their shoulders and continue to kidnap thousands more Ukrainian children against their will. There are reports and proof that some of these children have been sexually violated, raped, and tortured!"

Laryssa started to cry. "I want to stop this!" she sobbed. "All this horror. Children suffering. Many are sick! Devastated!"

She buried her face in her hands. "I still have my contacts in Sibiu. Romania is gathering evidence for The Hague. I will help. Kidnapping children is the quickest evidence to document crimes against humanity. Forcible transfer of children is against all laws . . ." She stopped talking.

I wondered was there a connection to her being in Sibiu as a student and her work today? Was she trying to tell me something?

As I was trying to put the puzzle together, Laryssa's phone rang.

She stood up, went into a corner, turned her back to me, and quietly spoke in Russian or Belarusian.

While waiting until she finished, I took off my heart locket with the intention of showing her the photo of my sons and husband, but I quickly decided not to. I didn't want her to ask what's on the other half of the heart—a Google app. The spy in her might suspect that my locket was a form of spyware and that I've been recording her words.

She returned, looking pensive and spoke in a lowered voice, "My daughter, Tanya, called me again. I feel I must go home to return her call while I'm alone. My husband is at a meeting . . ."

I didn't know if *alone* meant she wanted to be away from her husband to return Tanya's call.

"It's good my husband is not at home."

She shrugged her shoulders, obviously very tense, and also angry. I wondered if her expression meant that she was irritated with her husband. Was she giving me clues?

She looked at me as if she wanted to tell me more. But instead, she said in her controlled voice, "Please next time, I want to see photos of your sons but not right now. It's not that I want to leave, but . . ."

She looked at me with a strange expression of fear, as if she wanted to tell me why she didn't want to leave. But instead, she politely apologized. "I'm sorry."

She put several five-dollar bills on the table. I noticed it wasn't enough to pay the bill or tip. She had just left money for her own coffee. I put another ten-dollar bill next to hers as she rushed toward the swivel doors.

At that moment, I returned my attention to my coffee. I stared at the half-finished liquid, took a packet of sugar and with my spoon, stirred the white granules into the dark espresso.

In the spoon's reflection, I saw Laryssa open the door to leave. Suddenly, moving towards her, grabbing her arm, I saw reflected in my spoon, an image of a man. He was short, twice the width of Laryssa, filling up my spoon with his huge frame. But then I lost him as well as Laryssa. My spoon was too small for a larger view. I couldn't see if she had left with him. Willingly. Without violence.

I quickly got up from my chair and ran to the door. My instinct was to help her, but I didn't see them. I rushed into the street. They weren't there. I rushed to the corner. No one. I ran to the next street and the next. No one. I was thunderstruck.

CHAPTER 12

Plans for Mexico

There was a one-month intercession from my classes. My husband and I were preparing to visit my brother, James, and my sister-in-law, Hildie, in Tulum, Mexico, where they had just bought a beach house. Being warned that the wifi service was weak and often non-existent, I decided not to take my computer, and instead decided to rely on my cell phone for emails and text messages. I was on vacation, away from the cold and wind, and I wanted to enjoy myself. I was looking forward to visiting archeological sites and snorkeling every day. Why not, I kept reminding myself. I deserve a holiday.

As I was packing, I thought of Laryssa. I had received several emails from her since our last time at Café D'Oro. But she didn't speak of the burly man who had whisked her away. Frightened for her, as I wasn't sure if she went with him voluntarily or not, I thought it best not to bring up the incident. Instead, I turned my thoughts to our last conversation about film. She had said something strange.

"It's odd," I remember her confiding in me, "but today, my husband received an invitation to see the film, *Argentina 1985* at UN Headquarters in the Security Council. The invitation said, 'Private. Non-transferable.'

"I wonder why he received such an invitation," she wondered. "And why were they showing that film at the UN?

"That's a film you showed us last semester about Argentina's crimes against humanity," she reminded me. "I remember you had said that the Argentine prosecutor had initiated his investigation just days after the military junta was out and a democratic government had been voted in."

She continued to inform me in a strange voice, "You had told us that the process the prosecutor took to gather proofs and witnesses was inspired by the Trial of Nuremberg after World War II."

I recalled how distressed she was, talking about genocide and war crimes, which continued to be foremost in her mind. She was obsessed by a possible investigation.

I realized that it wasn't a coincidence that this Argentine film was being shown at the UN. It was a warning that the UN is preparing data against Belarus and Russia to prove crimes against humanity. Those invited to attend had been hand-picked to warn them of an imminent investigation against Russia and Belarus.

My maternal instinct was leading me to deny that she or her husband could ever be involved in such dealings. Yet, news reports were coming out about her country's involvement. Perhaps it was the writer in me that persisted in gathering pieces of a puzzle about my mysterious female protagonist.

I remembered when we were walking in the streets of New York, on Park Avenue, and the limo had tried to plow into us. Could I believe Laryssa's quick rationalization that it must have been a drunken driver? Was she trying to cover up something for my sake? She had appeared to be truly scared.

And Laryssa—what was inside her, without her mask of control?

I could tell that she was obsessed with being accused of war crimes. She had been part of the Belarusian administration for twenty years and was presently working with her husband, a leading general—part of the military, like Argentine's military. Was she afraid that in association with her husband, she might be judged by a tribunal and accused of crimes against humanity? She had reason to be scared. And I was scared for her.

Laryssa had confided to me about her love for Mexico. I thought she might be considering going into self-exile and living there. But a decision like that would surely have complications: her daughters. Is that why she had visited them—to discuss plans to get them to Mexico? Or out of Belarus?

Was she thinking which country, Russia or America, would protect her from a trial? Was she waiting to see which one would give her the best deal?

It was hard to know with her. And yet, I couldn't stop feeling compassion for her, and hoped she'd continue to stay strong.

Despite all her problems and all the signals of distress, I sensed she'd find an answer—a resolution to her conflict—perhaps in an unexpected way. I trusted her to do so. I was sure she wouldn't give up until she did.

PART 2

MEXICO

Winter, Spring, Summer 2023

CHAPTER 13

Vacation in Mexico

My brother sent his driver, Luis, to pick us up at the airport. Luis took my suitcase, which was a relief for my non-functional arm, and less of a burden for my husband who wanted to take my suitcase as well as his.

Luis guided us through the crowd, and I was beginning to feel my vacation mood as the warm air filled me with pleasure. I took a deep breath, knowing we'd be protected from now on, and allowed myself the comfort of Mexico's lovely climate.

We weren't sure how long we'd stay in this paradise. No plans were necessary, and we had decided to be flexible. Lodging was not a problem, and our work could be done remotely. I was still lecturing on Zoom and my husband, Gene, could do telemedicine while on vacation. All we wanted was for us to enjoy ourselves and be together.

Once in the car, Gene began practicing his Spanish with Luis, delighting in conversing more and more comfortably as we moved onto the highway. He had been studying Spanish in New York, preparing for our trip. I always admired the scholar in him, whatever he did.

I rolled down the rear window and leaned out to admire the palm trees with coconuts next to red sage bushes. The road sign in kilometers indicated the distance to Tulum and reminded me of collective vacations from the past. COVID had blocked our adventurous spirit, and I was delighted to have it reawakened once again. I was overwhelmed with the privilege of making up for lost pleasures. Travel had been a sort of an addiction for me.

Forty-five minutes later, Luis turned into a private entrance, stopped in front of security, showed his ID, and proceeded onto an unpaved, one-lane road. In front of a recently renovated house of white stone, surrounded by colorful orange honeysuckle bushes and clay pots with red dahlias, I saw my brother, James, waving his arm.

I hadn't seen James for the past three years, as he too, had been staying safely at home in Palm Springs, his residence of forty years. His curly ponytail was now streaked gray, and his stubbled chin was almost white. The sun shone on his straight frame, still tall and lean. He was wearing his ubiquitous long white shirt of Indian style with sun-bleached jeans and black rubber beach sandals. James had lived for thirteen years in Tibet, from 1967 to 1980—until the Chinese secured their power by declaring Tibet an autonomous region within the control of China. Foreigners were immediately suspect and escorted out.

Yet, after so many years in that beautiful country, James had considered himself a Buddhist Tibetan, a member of a lost tribe in a lost country he had loved.

The dominating Chinese did not agree with his beliefs. They dismantled his carpet factories in Lhasa where he had set up a school for women and had also conducted his export business. They placed him and his young family under house arrest and issued him a choice of a black jail in China or a chance to return to the States. He wisely accepted the latter, despite his reluctance to leave his successful business and dear friends.

Returning to New York, his hometown, he decided to venture west, and find a new residence that reminded him of the beauty he had to leave behind. It was Palm Springs that lured him, with its charm of mountains and desert. There he put his adventurous spirit to work. His business acumen told him that this city was special. A land of golden beauty and opportunity to explore.

He set up a store for his carpets and filled the rooms with treasures he had brought from Nepal, Bhutan, Mongolia, India, and Pakistan. He loved beauty and believed such a love could be transformed into a profitable life in Palm Springs. He started to buy real estate in the way that we used to play Monopoly as children. And he was on a roll; he sensed what was good, and what would become better.

His store's success on fashionable Palm Canyon Drive allowed him profits to buy a small hotel that he hand-decorated in the style of a waystation from the Himalayan mountains of Tibet. Room by room, with colorful fabrics on the ceilings in caftan style, Dhurrie carpets on tiled floors, bathrooms decorated with mosaics, cloisonné vases filled with crystal minerals, and Buddhists' chests filled with prayer beads for good luck, he recreated what he had to leave behind. A lost world of magic, a kaleidoscope of color and exoticism. The public loved it!

His inn became worthy of pilgrimages and retreats, and soon it was converted and coveted as a *Relais & Chateau*. Success was his as he worked diligently, day by day, to keep his creations artistic and special.

The house on the beach on the Mayan Riviera of Mexico was his reward.

* * *

James helped us with our bags and led us to the backyard beach. Proudly, he gave us a tour of his manor.

It was more than a simple beach house. James had told us that the long-time owners were the original developers of the pueblo. They were aristocratic Mexicans from the capital, who had wanted a retreat for their family of three children and grandchildren. They chose a location that overlooked the entire bay and constructed four adjoining townhouses with a swimming pool in the center, surrounded by groves of coconut trees.

Each townhouse consisted of four bedrooms built on two stories with expanding terraces. The interiors were furnished with rattan straw chairs and sofas, covered in multi-colored Mexican fabrics and touches of colorful ceramics. Multiple windows and glass sliding doors allowed the sun to brighten the interior all day. The four houses were attached, but without any entry from one to the other. It was ideal for James and his three sons—separate but together.

When we returned to the front door of James' house, he saw his neighbor, who was arranging swimming gear in his four-wheel-drive Range Rover. He was alone, wearing shorts, a T-shirt, and sandals.

"Alexey! Alexey, my friend," James yelled to his neighbor in his extroverted way. "Come meet my sister, Sybil and her husband, Dr. Gene Edwards."

Alexey approached us, shook our hands, and said several words of welcome. After a few pleasantries, he turned to James and invited us all to join him for a swim in one of the Mayan springs, called *Cenote*. We quickly agreed. My sister-in-law, Hildie, had left for the afternoon to do some errands, so we wrote her a note in case she wanted to join us.

Alexey was wearing a baseball cap that had an American flag on the brim. I studied it but was quickly taken with his deep blue eyes the color of the sky. His smile was charming, and he carried his tall body gracefully, as if he had been an athlete in his youth. He was blond with a touch of silver gray at the temples. He spoke with a slight accent that I was unable to guess the origins of, but I found intriguing. Above all, he was extremely handsome, suntanned to a golden hue. He looked like a movie star.

Alexey opened the back of his car to show my brother an icon that he had recently found and bought in an outdoor market near Cancun.

My brother, loving anything exotic, held it up to the sun to admire its beauty. "How lovely. What a find," James agreed. "Looks like eighteenth-century Russian."

"I think so." Alexey and James shared an appreciation of eastern antiques and foreign cultures. "I wonder how a Russian icon found its way to Cancun," Alexey said. "I hope a Russian didn't hock it for vodka."

They both laughed. There was a mutual admiration that passed from one to the other as they continued to chat about other Russian artifacts that Alexey had found at a flea market nearby.

"There must be a good number of thirsty Russians in the area," my brother said, jokingly.

"Probably. I hope I don't encounter them when they're drunk," Alexey replied. "How strange is the route of antiques that go from one country to another. A diaspora and its people can be traced by art. It's a mystery that I love to unfold."

Then my brother turned to me and commented, "Alexey is from Minsk, the same city as our three grandparents."

"Minsk!" I tried hard to control my enthusiasm—not because of my ancestry, but because of my friend.

"Oh!" was all I could say. But my mind went into gear. He was about the same age as Laryssa—fifty—and Minsk is not a large city. I wondered if coincidences do happen. I smiled and allowed my enthusiasm to show.

I quickly said, "Minsk . . . I have a friend in New York who lives in Minsk. Goes back and forth all the time. Presently, she's in New York, and her husband works at the UN. He's a general, Belarus's military attaché."

"Really?" Alexey stared at me. "Maybe I know her. What's her name?"

"Laryssa Pavlovich."

It was as if I had struck him over the head with one of his icons.

"You must be joking!" he said in disbelief. His body bent forward, appearing broken.

"No, I'm not." I felt like moving away, afraid he'd lose his balance and fall on me.

"What does she look like?" he asked as if he needed proof that we were talking about the same person.

"She's very beautiful, tall, thin, high Slavic cheek bones, blue eyes, and above all, blazing, curly red hair."

He said nothing; instead, he moved away and went to his car to sit down. I stared at him, alone in his Range Rover. After several seconds, he regained his composure and got out of his car. "Yes, I know her."

Recapturing his self-control, he said to my brother, "So, James, how about we go for a swim? I feel like cooling off a little. Can you all be ready in ten minutes?"

CHAPTER 14

Coincidences Don't Just Happen

We sat in Alexey's Range Rover with the hood and windows down. I felt like an explorer protected by three handsome men. James was in the front next to Alexey who was driving; Gene and I in the rear. Gene was busy entertaining us by talking about the varied plant life he noticed along the roadside. It reminded him of photos in botany books that he had read as a student.

Eugene, known to everyone as Gene, had been raised and educated in Bucharest, Romania, during the horrendous times of fascism and then communism. Growing up under two horrific regimes, he had found comfort in his books. He became a doctor, but because his grandfather had been a landowner and his father a doctor—bourgeois according to communist authorities—he was not allowed to practice medicine in any city. Instead, he was sent to the countryside. He considered that a life of exile.

He'd tell me stories of how cold the winters were—a glass of water at his bedside would turn to ice by morning; and muddy paths that his horse and buggy could never pass through. Hard times, except for the pleasure of practicing medicine that he loved. Helping patients, despite his limited equipment and non-existent medicines, was the highlight of his life in Romania.

One day, a Romani came to the clinic. She claimed she did not have a chicken or egg or bottle of wine for payment, but she had the gift of the divine. She could read palms—tell him his future.

"You will soon make a long trip. Go far away on a boat. And be happy."

Gene worked and worked until the prophecy came true and New York City became more than a dream.

He and I met by chance—he picked me up in Central Park as our bikes collided on a sunny, autumn afternoon. How strange it had been—I fell in love with him at that moment. How was that possible? Was it fate? Coincidences just don't happen. I believed it was a miracle.

The rest is history: a loving marriage of many decades, two sons, the ups and downs of life, and partners to the end.

Gene understood me, shared my tribulations and goals. His strength was steadfast, and he gave me the unrequited love I had not received as a child growing up. We shared everything that we did—sports, travel, books, nature—a thirst for life. Each day was another pleasure. There was never a his or hers that came to mind. Values and morals were the same as we agreed to do our best.

And my added perk was that Gene was so good looking. Blue eyes, blond hair, not too tall, not too thin, just right. Above all, he had a laugh and optimism that had conquered me. That I had needed. He was sensitive and strong, realistic yet dreamy. He was a gentleman in every sense of the term. My anchor. I was a lucky woman.

We listened intently as Gene explained how all kinds of leaves and berries were used in native civilizations to fight against diseases of the heart, lungs, and stomach. And he smiled, devilishly, while teasing us with the words, "Poisons. Evil that turns red blood to black."

The gastroenterologist in him was amazed at the abundance of different plants in the open jungles we were passing by.

I was quiet, listening to Gene's stories of which plants are used for medicine, and then to James and Alexey who turned the conversation to gold from Mayan times.

Alexey entertained us with a story of an auction he had just attended in Washington, D.C., where he had been living for more than thirty years. My brother had told me that Alexey used his house in Tulum sporadically, when he wasn't busy doing whatever else he was doing besides eyeing and buying treasures.

As I listened to Alexey chatter of this and that, I noticed that he was avoiding speaking of his real work—what he did to finance his pleasures. He was a mysterious man, this handsome Alexey. He must have his secrets.

My brother had given me a rundown about what he knew about Alexey when we were preparing our swim gear and snorkels.

"Alexey has been divorced from his wife, Sonya, for many years. They never had children. Living alone, he has dedicated his life to collecting art, which gives him an excuse to travel away from Washington, D.C., usually to countries like Moldova, Georgia, Serbia, Ukraine, and Russia, where

Orthodox priests are willing to fill their war chests with dollars and sell hidden treasures."

I listened to my brother as he spoke of his friend, and quietly I absorbed each detail. After all, I'm a writer and I brought my notebook with me.

I had consciously planned to work on my spy thriller while in Mexico. But now, with Alexey, reacting so strongly about Laryssa, I considered adding some chapters for a love story. Spies and passion mix well together. Politics and love make a good sub plot. And I realized that unexpected details were falling in my lap. Nuggets of gold from the golden Mayan coast.

I would put my imagination to work.

My brother continued his story.

"Alexey's grandfather was an artist, one of Belarus's modernists. He founded the Vitebsk Arts College with his friend, Marc Chagall. They both were born in Vitebsk, a city 140 miles from Minsk. It was part of Russia then, and now Belarus. Together, they introduced the modernistic style in painting.

"When Chagall left Belarus for Paris, Alexey's grandfather inherited the art school as well as three Chagall paintings that were hidden in the basement. He passed down the cubist oils to his only grandchild, Alexey. Several years ago, Alexey sold one of them at auction to buy his dream house on the beach."

My brother smiled, thinking of his friend. "Alexey and I share a love for art and beauty. A good basis for friendship. And now we're neighbors. He's advising me on how to enclose my property with a stone wall. It's my winter project."

My brother never failed to intrigue me—he always needed a project. He was a character like no one else. My husband claimed that as brother and sister we were very much alike—a diagnosis that I was reluctant to accept. Sibling rivalry from early years had colored our relationship, as James had taken more of my parents' attention. Two years older than me, he was always first, and I had resented his *right of seigneur*. Yes, my husband's diagnosis was true—both of us were strong-willed and had rebelled against a society that we did not want to make our own.

Our father found himself bankrupt when James was fifteen and I was thirteen—vulnerable years for such trauma. We had to leave our house, which was quickly under-sold, and move into the homes of family and friends—for no rent at all—to finish high school. James, however, as a poor student, abandoned academic learning in favor of the streets. I was sent to my grandparents. My only recourse was my books, while James found his salvation in making money.

Never liking school, and not returning ever to study, money became his lifeline even at a young age. What kept him inspired was his need to have more and more. Insatiable, he never had enough. I, on the other hand, found a home in books—my citadel of the imaginary where I could escape and survive.

Our parents relocated to Florida after leaving us to find our own way. Eventually, we did. Perhaps, that's what my husband had observed that we had in common—a strength and yet a fear to leave our anchors, whether books or money—and a panic we'd sink without them. The angst kept us struggling and achieving while never giving up. Some people viewed it with admiration—they saw it as ambition, a creative force. We saw it as a cover up, a way to feed a hungry ego and obliterate the past.

My husband was so different from James and myself—a luckier mold of stability because he had been so loved. As an only child, he had been protected despite totalitarian regimes in the middle of hell, while James and I just had hell.

Our consolation was that James and I had learned a talent to survive. We learned it from the streets, and we were not afraid of obstacles. This I accepted as the only compensation for a difficult beginning in life.

I stared at Alexey driving his Range Rover and wondered what his life in Minsk had been. My brother had told me that Alexey had to leave Belarus at eighteen when his father secretly left for the States. Why Washington, D.C., I wondered. And Alexey was still living there. There must be something besides auction houses and collecting art that needs his attention.

I wondered if it was chance that Alexey was my brother's neighbor. That he was born in Minsk? Lived in Washington, D.C.?

I believe there's no such thing as coincidences. I believe in fate, destiny. What was meant to be was meant to be. "*La certitude du hazard.*"

It seemed pretty clear that Alexey knew Laryssa quite well from his reaction. I wondered what would happen if she actually came to visit us from Cancun? Should I arrange it? I was playing with the idea of inviting her to join us for a lunch or dinner on the beach. I'd insist that she come alone. I was hoping that she'd agree to pay us a social call without her husband.

* * *

We had placed our towels on chaises lounges at the edge of a mineral pool where we were swimming. We now wiped ourselves dry, and Alexey asked us if we wanted a tour of the Mayan ruins through the nearby jungle. Delighted, we put on our sandals and wrapped our towels on our shoulders to follow him.

Footpaths, made over the centuries, were covered with crushed coral and limestone while marked paths followed the mineral lagoon. Every few minutes, an iguana would cross in front of our feet and hide among the banana trees in camouflage. Paths twisted and turned, even mounted several feet above the pools of mineral water and I imagined how much fun it was for a child to swing from a tree into the pool.

Alexey paused at a patch of wild mushrooms. He took a stick and pointed to several spotted red mushrooms next to solid yellow ones.

"These mushrooms have magical powers, so I've been told." He smiled as he took some in his hand. "Many of the male elders in Mayan country, make a tea with these after dinner. They claim the mushrooms increase potency."

Gene bent down to study them. "Maybe these magic mushrooms carry the secret of anti-aging," he said, laughing.

Hildie and I bent down to study them, also. We all smiled, wondering.

After hiking a half hour, we returned to our lounge chairs, and as a reward had another dip in the mineral pool. Then, there was a surprise snack that Alexey had arranged. He served us cheese and crackers with a white Spanish wine, which he had placed in the pool to cool. We chatted and laughed, enjoying the magic of the Mayan lagoon.

I marveled at the crystal-clear water, the clean floor of shells and crushed coral, and I tried to figure out how many centuries all this has remained the same. I wondered, was it still as safe and tranquil in this paradise as it had been before. Or will modernity bring a surprise?

CHAPTER 15

A New Toy with a New Surprise; The Devil Lurks in Still Waters; Dining Amidst Russian Threats; Mysterious Alexey

---

The next morning, as Gene and I were having our morning coffee, Hildie came knocking at our door. She held in her arms a large machine, very heavy. She smiled as she described what she was carrying. For her it appeared rather light, but when I picked it up, its weight pulled me forward. She helped me before I and the machine could fall down. I had problems holding an object weighing more than five pounds.

"A Christmas gift from our boys. We have two machines to be used when snorkeling. This will propel you forward even while you're wearing flippers and mask."

And she pointed out its features. "Here's the motor and these are the handlebars to control the speed. When you release your finger, here, the machine stops, very suddenly, and you'll have to be careful not to lose your balance."

I assured her that I could do it—even with my one functional arm.

"The water will make the machine feel light weight for you. Just kick your feet and float. How about we try it after breakfast? From our beach, the coral is beautiful, and we'll see scores of tropical fish."

How could I refuse?

Several hours later, Hildie was all prepared with her snorkeling gear and machines. She twisted her long blond hair into a bun and put on her water shoes so as not to be cut by the coral. With her strong body, several inches taller than me, she plunged into the water. Yelling from the waves, she told me, "Take the machine. Do exactly the same as me. Make sure to follow me."

I jumped in the water, all geared up, and was absolutely enthralled. I allowed the magic machine to propel me forward to glide through the sea for new colors and wonders.

Striped fish—blues, reds, oranges, yellows, rainbow, small and large—flowed in and out of coral shaped fans. The magic of an underworld that I had never known before.

The snorkeling machine was a pleasure—a new toy propelling me forward with little effort from my arms or legs. My only concern was not to drift too far away from Hildie.

But I did go far, without realizing it.

Skimming the water, I followed one school of fish after another not concerned about time or place, just indulging myself in a new pleasure that I could do without effort. Until I felt the sea beneath me shake.

I lifted my head out of the water, took off my snorkeling mask, and noticed a power boat approaching me. I smelled something burning. The sea made waves that shook me.

A bald, heavy-set man was throwing flares at me. I knew from my sailing days that flares were fired to send a distress signal. I looked around, but there was no boat that needed help. In fact, there were no other boats in the area.

The bald man was at the bow, lighting flares, throwing the flames at me. Dozens of fiery flares!

I swam quickly away, hoping my weak arm would be able to match the speed of my legs. I kicked harder and harder. He had a friend who kept throwing flares at me and their boat kept getting nearer and nearer. I swam as fast as I could and pressed Hildie's machine to its maximum.

As I was struggling, I heard them yell into large bullhorns, while laughing at the same time. In a thick Russian accent, they shouted, "I hope we scared you! Tell your neighbor he's next. And he won't get away like you!"

I saw their boat turn speed away.

At that moment, I heard my brother yell, "You went too far! Thank God, I found you!"

I wondered if he had seen the power boat following me and targeting me with flares.

James was in his kayak, telling me that he had been searching for me. He reprimanded me that I had gone too far away from his beach, and he pointed to the area where I should have been snorkeling.

As the big brother and father of three, he signaled for me to return to safer quarters. He turned his kayak around and I followed him, swimming to the section that was certainly further away from where I had started.

James guided me on his kayak to make sure I knew the way, while explaining his concern. "There was a boat following you. Going very fast—making huge waves—must have been an expensive kind, a cigarette, not allowed in these waters. Only small fishing boats should be here. And then I saw fire being hurled at you. I knew I needed to get you! Fast!"

Gene and Hildie were waiting for us at their beach. My husband said he was worried and Hildie, with her maternal instinct, was relieved to see me.

Alexey, from the neighboring beach, came over to see what the commotion was all about. Eyeing the snorkeling machine, he asked if he could try it. My brother warned him of the dangerous speed boat that was roaming the waters. "The likes of which, I've never seen before. Going as fast as a race car. With an unusual flag for these waters—red, blue and white stripes with a gold eagle in the middle."

"Russian," I heard Alexey mumble, and saw his golden-hued face turn pale. He looked concerned. "Well, maybe another time I'll go snorkeling. How about lunch, instead? I invite you all. There's a new hotel nearby where the chef is getting great reviews."

I decided not to give Alexey the Russian's message until after lunch. Why frighten him that he might be next?

* * *

Alexey insisted on taking his Range Rover with the top and windows opened to the air. "I love the feel of the wind," he said, smiling. "Can't get that during the winter in Washington."

His words reminded me where he lived—the writer in me took note. A detail to return to.

We approached the restaurant's gatehouse. Two Mexican security guards carrying machine guns and wearing a belt filled with bullets, asked us if we have a reservation. Alexey answered no. They searched the car, the trunk also. They remarked my large, brimmed straw hat and the men's baseball caps and figured we were *gringos*—tourists. With a move from his machine gun, the shorter, stronger one, waved us on.

The entrance road was at least as long as several Manhattan streets. At each turn, there was another security guard with another automatic rifle in warning. At the end of the line, there was a tall, stone pillar holding a Buddha statue—I wondered if it were there to offer us good luck.

Rows of palm trees and exotic flowering bushes paralleled our path. Bordering them, were groves of banana trees, lined with cages of exotic parrots perched on brass stands that appeared golden in the sun. Five minutes after this dramatic entry, we were greeted by several women dressed in Indian saris with wide bare midriffs and bursting breasts. I saw all my men smile at the same time.

Alexey stopped his jeep where the staff indicated, and in his charming manner, greeted the beautiful women with, "*Hola, amigas. Qué lindas están.*"

They bowed in response and Alexey, smiling, stood straighter with their approval.

The maître d' appeared, said his pleasantries and escorted us to a corner table overlooking the sea. The beach was perfectly clean, as was the azul water surrounding it. The scene was like a picture-perfect tourist card with parasols and chaises lounges next to straw tables displayed with fruits and drinks.

The waiter told us there were no menus, just the whim of the chef for the day. "Is that ok?" We turned to Alexey, our host. He smiled and responded, "How could I say no."

The only table occupied was in the opposite corner of the restaurant, which was not quite far away enough to dismiss their loud chatter. Four heavy-set men were seated, speaking gruffly in a foreign language, smoking pungent cigars. On their table were two bottles of Dom Perignon Rosé champagne. One man, the oldest of the group, was dressed in white, wearing a white Borsalino hat and very large, dark sunglasses. He appeared somewhat secretive, looking around, puffing his cigar.

Next to him was another mysterious character. He was wearing a straw hat, white suit and black tie—very out of place at the beach.

At their table were two bald musclemen. One was dressed in a black T-shirt with a small black scarf tied tightly knotted around his neck. I stared at the knot of his scarf and stroked my neck.

I tried not to acknowledge him; he looked so frightening. He must have been the bodyguard.

The waiter brought us the first dish, compliments from the chef. "These are his *amuse-bouches*, appetizers to welcome you," he told us.

Little puffs of fried dough stuffed with *foie gras* melted in our mouths. Alexey was the first to finish and express his delight. "The chef must be French. Someone paid him dearly to come here."

I thought the same thing as I looked around at the plush surroundings. All the tables but two were empty of clients; and yet, the placings were set with Baccarat wine glasses and Limoges dishes. I imagined the chef was properly compensated although business was nil. I was relieved to think that Alexey was enjoying himself and not worrying about the bill.

The sommelier approached us, handing Alexey the wine list. We all declined.

"Thank you but no, not during the day."

"I still want to swim after lunch."

"Too early for me."

But Alexey noticed a Chateau Lafitte 1989. "I must take it—an omen—it will bring us good luck—a good year that meant a lot to me."

After a couple of glasses, Alexey was relaxing.

Turning to my brother, he asked James, "Where were you in 1989?"

James replied, "In Palm Springs. It had been years since I had left Tibet and Lhasa."

"And you, Gene?"

"I had left Romania—struggling in New York to build up a Park Avenue, GI practice."

"I was still in Minsk," Alexey said, sipping his glass of wine. "It wasn't until the next year that my father decided to leave. Or, should I say, it was decided for him."

Alexey paused, took another sip, and commented, "Your government made the decision for him. He was on your side."

We all remained silent, realizing he was implying the CIA. But as Alexey was beginning to feel the wine, and open himself up to talk, we waited and remained quiet. I was hoping to hear more; I was taking mental notes.

Turning to me, he asked, without any warning or logic, "Sybil, please tell me about you friend, Laryssa. Tell me anything. Anything." Then he paused, "Above all, does she seem happy?"

He closed his eyes, his face tightened, his head tilted down. His body language said it all. I understood.

"She's very reserved. Controlled. Hard to know what she thinks or feels. I don't think happiness is one of her goals."

Alexey nodded his head. "She was always like that, as if there was a separation of her mind and soul. She chose to do what she had to do, not what her heart wanted. She was ambitious."

He turned to James. "Ambitious, but not for money. Not even for power. For something else. Harder to get. I could never figure out what. I wished it would have been my love."

So moved by his words, I was tempted to pour myself a glass from his Chateau Lafitte bottle, but I froze. I felt his sorrow.

"I was never able to love another woman after losing Laryssa." He put his face in his hands.

Gene took his arm. The doctor in him tried to reassure the suffering man.

Alexey continued. "We were students together at the university. She had just relocated from St. Petersburg to Minsk to pursue a more western curriculum. We met there the very first day of class. I came without a notebook or paper or pen. She smiled to me, her beautiful smile, and I couldn't stop myself from asking, 'Would you share with me what you have? So foolish of me to come unprepared.'

"I fell in love with her at that very moment."

He was clearly moved.

"She was my first woman. I was her first man. We were so young, before everything . . ."

His pause was as painful as his words.

"We were together every day, taking the same classes. We were together every night. I had a small studio in the student dorm. She was so beautiful, my goddess . . ." He stopped talking.

Gene took his arm again and asked, "What happened when you left for the States?"

"I asked her to marry me. Come with me, I begged. Leave Belarus. My father said he'd arrange it all. He loved her like a daughter. But she refused. She said she couldn't. She had obligations. She had to do what was right. She couldn't think only of herself."

"Did you ever see her again?" James asked. He, too, was a romantic, like Gene and me.

"I wrote to her, phoned her, pleaded with her for several years to join me. She said she couldn't leave her family. She refused to explain. And that was that. No, I never saw her again. I never stopped loving her."

Then he said, "It would take a miracle for me to find her."

"But miracles happen!" I said to him in a soft voice.

"Not for me." He wiped his eyes.

I wanted to cry with him. Then I remembered that Laryssa had said something about a miracle. She wished for a miracle—to find the man she loved.

Alexey poured himself another glass of wine, finishing the bottle. He was ready to continue to empty himself of pain when he turned to the table in the corner that was making a good deal of noise.

The man with the white Borsalino hat stood up. He took his glass and threw champagne in the face of the man in the white suit. The two bodyguards stood up, grabbed the man with the white suit. Held him tight, pushed him down into his seat. They were all arguing loudly, but I couldn't decipher their words.

Alexey turned toward them, shouted at them in their language, Russian, and they stopped; they were shocked. Angry at the interference, the man with the Borsalino hat took his bodyguard's half-empty glass and threw the remaining champagne at Alexey's feet.

The muscleman with the black scarf knotted around his neck, stood up, walked over to Alexey, and took out a gun. But he quickly put it back when two guards from the restaurant approached him with their automatic rifles.

Alexey whispered, "Oh no. Could it be him?" The bodyguard with the black knot around his neck looked familiar to Alexey.

The maître d' ran toward Alexey to prevent him from fighting back. Two more security guards appeared and blocked Alexey. The maître d' went to the other table to quiet the men, speaking first in Spanish, then in English. The man with the white Borsalino hat stood up and put a wad of hundred-dollar bills on the table. He signaled to the others to follow him and before they stormed out of the restaurant, he yelled to Alexey in English, "No one tells me to shut up!"

The muscleman with the black scarf flashed his pistol at Alexey and yelled in Russian, "We'll meet again. Remember that!"

Alexey didn't react, didn't move a muscle, didn't say a word. Instead, he calmly flagged the waiter, asked in Spanish when our next dish would be ready, and ordered a glass of scotch.

And that was that. I remembered how Laryssa often ended a difficult conversation with, "That's life."

Several minutes passed. The steam of angry words had been quieted down. Alexey was calm and talkative, surprisingly so, and quite in control. I thought about how strong he was—he must have gone through a lot in his life to have such restraint.

We gave our attention to our dish of langouste and shrimp and sent our compliments to the chef.

Chatting like nothing had happened to upset us, we spoke of this and that. Then I got enough courage to ask Alexey if he knew Laryssa's friend, the foreign minister, Makei.

He nodded his head. "Our best friend at the university. We were a trio. On weekends we went skiing together or played tennis. Vlad was a great pianist. There was a bistro near the university where we'd go every evening after dinner. Vlad would play the piano and Laryssa would sing. She had a beautiful voice. She was so happy singing, so full of life. Vlad was happy playing for her . . ."

He paused, closing his eyes as if he was reliving her songs. "She liked American music, rock 'n' roll, and theme songs from movies." Alexey became emotional.

We all waited for him to steady himself. He ordered dessert. We waited. Then, he continued. "Vlad was also a linguist. He spoke several languages. His greatest pleasure was to get up early in the morning and go to a newsstand near the university where they sold foreign newspapers: English, French, German. Before six in the morning, there were no secret police to monitor it.

"Vlad would grab the papers, take them home, and devour each one while he had breakfast. He used to give us a summary of the world news in the evening, at our little bistro. Then he'd play the piano and Laryssa would sing."

"Did you see Vlad after you left Minsk?" I asked in a whisper. I was starting to think and act like a spy.

"Yes, I saw Vlad. Laryssa, never, never again." He took a sip of his scotch.

"I saw Vlad often over the years in Washington. As foreign minister, he was sent to D.C. to confer with each American administration for the Belarusian government."

"Lukashenko allowed these trips?" Gene asked, surprised.

"Yes and no. He never knew the details. All he knew was that he had sent his foreign minister to meetings in Washington to discuss global affairs with American officials. What Vlad did after hours, the boss never knew. That was done off any schedule or protocol, without press, in top secret, without anyone knowing.

"Sometimes Vlad would have private, off-the-record dinners at the White House or at the Pentagon, and with me . . ." Alexey paused again, giving out morsels of information. I clung to each word.

"Vlad was our bridge," Alexey stated in the same hushed voice he had used before.

Did I dare ask who ours was? Dare I ask how Vlad had died?

Gene, my better half, asked the question. "Was he poisoned?" The doctor in him wanted to know the cause of death.

Alexey stared at Gene and blinked his eyes at the inquiry. But he didn't answer.

"Must have been poisoned," Gene replied for Alexey. "A Russian trademark."

Alexey shrugged his shoulders and didn't say a word. It was apparent he was well trained not to divulge such details.

"Why poisoned?" my brother asked. Until now James had been quiet, but he thought of the plants across the road from his house—a vacant lot, a jungle that he was planning to buy. Full of plants, some good, some bad. His gardener had pointed to the poisonous ones, telling him, "Beware." James wasn't sure he should buy the land.

"Why was he poisoned?" Alexey repeated. "A warning," he answered to his own question.

We all said at once, "To whom?"

"To anyone working with Ukraine. To make sure they understand to stay loyal to Belarus and Russia."

"Who in particular?" Gene asked again. He needed a better diagnosis.

"To Laryssa." Alexey coughed, taking a sip of water. "I hope she knows. I wish I could warn her. Help her. She could be next."

Gene put his arm around Alexey's shoulders.

I almost slipped off my chair. I placed my feet solidly on the ground and gave a painful sigh. Did that mean that I had been right all along? My friend was a spy! On our side. A mole! I prayed that Lukashenko didn't know.

Alexey's warning sounded true to me. A double agent is high risk. She could be in trouble. I had to do something.

"Alexey, I know how to find her."

He stared at me. "What are you talking about? Find her, how?" He stopped talking, confused.

"I will try to contact her."

I didn't say that I had her email and cell number. I didn't say that she was in Cancun. I wasn't sure what I would say to Alexey or Laryssa or how to explain what I was scheming. I only knew I had promised Laryssa that I would do everything I could to help her. I had shaken her hand. I told her I believe in miracles.

This was the moment to fulfill my promise and my role as a friend.

CHAPTER 16

Donkey with a Mystical Rose; Russian Roulette; Pegasus Spyware

---

As Alexey was driving to the highway, he took a small road by mistake. He didn't realize his error until he saw a donkey appear in front of his jeep. The animal was being led by a Mexican boy.

"*Mira, hombre, cuidado!* Careful!" The strongly built boy screamed and raised his hand to stop the car. In an angry tone, he pointed to his animal.

Alexey slammed on the brakes, apologized, and waited for the boy and donkey to cross the road.

"My fault," Alexey apologized; he was clearly upset by the situation.

"The boy reminded me of something from my past," Alexey explained. "A boy in a foreign city. I lost my concentration by staring at him."

"No problem," we consoled him. I realized that Alexey had finished the entire bottle of wine alone and shouldn't be driving. "Would you like me to take the wheel?" I asked him.

"No, it's ok. I can manage. But what you can do for me, is let me tell you about why I was startled by the boy. It's about Laryssa. There's no one else who knows her. I feel like I must talk to somebody."

"Of course." I was more than intrigued to provide him with an audience.

Alexey explained as he left the dirt road for the highway.

"Laryssa and I took a vacation together during our first year at the university during May 1st Workers' Day. It was 1990 in Budapest, the beginning of Spring. So exciting as communism was falling in Eastern Europe after 1989.

"We took the train from Minsk very early in the morning. We were so excited. It was the first time both of us had left our country and we were going on vacation together.

"The train stopped at Keleti Station, the end of the line in Budapest. I took Laryssa's hand, and we ran and ran, feeling so free. All the time, I felt as if we were movie characters who had passed through a black-and-white screen into a technicolored world. Minsk had been so dreary, so poor, so cold, while Budapest, despite just waking up from communism, was so alive! Even the weather was warmer. I couldn't believe the vibrant colors in the city as we neared the Chain Bridge.

"Turning my eyes upward to a blue sky, so free of smog, I saw the colored tiles of Matthias Church and seven white stoned turrets of Fisherman's Bastion. Below us was the Danube River, a greenish blue, winding like a snake, dividing the city into a left and right bank—the old section of *Buda* and the new *Pest.* Its serpentine waters called to us, and we ran toward it.

"Laryssa touched some green bushes and red flowers to make sure they were real. She looked through a clean window and wriggled her nose at her own image. She laughed and laughed while swaying her face back and forth to the window. She didn't even notice that people were staring at her.

"At the foot of the bridge, I spied a rose bush. Putting my nose next to the flowers, I was thrilled to smell their scent. They were real. I had never seen a rose with such a pink color. I looked around to ensure no one was watching, then picked the biggest one and gave it to Laryssa. 'Real like you. Sweet like the perfume from your lips.' I kissed her as she smelled it. I loved her so much!

"She rubbed its velvet layers on her cheek and then, closing her eyes, she threw the flower into the Danube and watched the flower float away.

"Laryssa started to run as if she wanted to follow the pink rose. I watched her as she waved to the Danube like a friend. We skipped back and forth on the Chain Bridge, touching the metal cables to make sure they were real. Back and forth, over and over again, we ran, only to stop to admire the river sparkling like diamonds in the sun.

"We were mesmerized by the panorama of roofs below us, marveling at the reality of sites that only yesterday were dots on the map we had studied.

"There was a boy at the end of the bridge. He was holding a donkey in the middle of the city. He didn't look real, but he was real, and he was holding a basket filled with roses of all colors. He took a white rose, gave it to Laryssa, and said to her, 'I wish you love. I wish you the miracle of loving together, forever.' He pointed to me and gave me a pink rose . . ."

Alexey paused, moved slowly off the highway, stopped at a side road, and waited for his tears to clear until he could see clearly.

* * *

Once in control, Alexey returned to the highway for Tulum. Upon entering the gated community, he showed the two guards his photo ID. They checked his license plate and waved him through with their rifles.

Suddenly, Alexey saw from his rear-view mirror a red Ferrari zooming up behind him. The driver pulled next to Alexey at the driver's side and started yelling at him. Alexey wasn't sure what he was saying, but he recognized the driver as the muscled bodyguard from the restaurant. He was the one with the black scarf knotted tightly around his neck. He yelled again at Alexey in English and then in Russian.

"Pig! I know your name," the driver shouted. "Alexey Simonovich! You're an enemy of our country! We know where your allegiance is. You'll pay for that!"

Alexey accelerated his speed. The Ferrari chased him. Alexey sped through the town at maximum speed. People on the street ran to the side; several cyclists were knocked down.

Alexey pulled into a driveway that was part of the Naval Control Board. A security guard came out of his stand, ready with his rifle, but then he recognized Alexey at the wheel. Alexey rolled down his window and pointed to the Ferrari following him.

"Get rid of him!" Alexey told the guard. "He's dangerous. A killer!"

The driver of the Ferrari shouted again at Alexey, "I know who you are!" He took his pistol and shot several bullets in the air as a warning.

At that second, Alexey told us, "I know who he is. I remember a photo that one of my colleagues showed me in Washington. He's a hit man working for Lukashenko.

"And he's well-connected, being protected by a cousin whose name I don't know but is high in the Belarusian government. The CIA is looking for him. His name is on their Wanted List with his photo—Boris Antonovich.

"I wonder what he's doing in Mexico. And who's his cousin?"

Alexey explained to us: "The Mexican president is anti-American, pro-Russian. But what is the Mexican government doing with Russians? Are they preparing something together? And now they know where I live."

But before Alexey could say anything further, the Ferrari and Russians sped away.

***

Upon arriving home, I looked for Hildie, with the hope that we could go for a swim—in her pool—alone. I needed to cool off. The car chase had shaken me. I realized the men in the car were after Alexey for a very specific reason, most likely political. I didn't know what it was. And I wondered if they were the same thugs who had thrown flares at me while I was swimming. They had yelled that Alexey would be next.

I certainly hoped Alexey wouldn't have more trouble with them. The first thing was for me was to contact Laryssa. I was afraid she could be the next one in danger. Alexey had feared the same—maybe with the same group of thugs.

But Hildie joined me at the pool and delayed me a few more minutes from texting Laryssa. "How was lunch?" she asked. "Sorry I missed it."

I answered that it was best that she had missed it. My remark only piqued her curiosity. After my explanation, she went into the house to get her phone and tell me that while she was waiting for us, she had been reading a report about Russians on the "Mayan coast," which included Cancun to southern Tulum as far as Chichi Itza. The article described the Russian mafia's presence in Mexico: not only for drug trafficking, but also for using Mexico as a center to get to Florida and then to Cuba through the waters and on to South America through the jungles. The goal was human trafficking.

Hildie reminded me that human trafficking was lucrative—migrants would pay anything to get a path through Mexico to the States. Fortunes were being made with the wrong people. And killings.

She pressed me to read the article before I did anything else. Politely, I said "yes" and put off contacting Laryssa.

My sister-in-law, Hildie, was German-born, raised in East Germany near Dresden. She had lost her accent as a child, as she came to the States at ten years old. The only remainder of her German heritage was her long golden hair that she wore in braids. She looked like the character Rapunzel from the German fairytale that I had enjoyed when I was a child.

Hilde had once told me that her mother was born a princess but had to renounce the title when she became an American citizen. Hildie, tall and slender, inherited an aristocratic carriage and maintained her bearing as a lady.

She worked closely with my brother, overseeing the marketing and publicity of their enterprises. But what she enjoyed the most was to wander through neighboring towns with her camera, in California or in Mexico, and take photos of children while they were playing. A talented photographer, her photos decorated the walls of their inn.

I was very fond of her and always enjoyed her company. When she eagerly wanted me to read now about the Russian Mafia on the Mexican coast, I couldn't refuse her.

Instead of letting me read from her phone, Hildie read it to me. In between paragraphs, she'd comment, interjecting the news with her opinion and what she knew personally.

"Listen to this," she started. "Russians are selling hordes of weapons to the Mexican government that can be used against anyone who stops the migrant flow to the border. Mexican officials are making their percentage with illegal migrants going to Texas and the Southwest and they need weapons to protect themselves against American security guards. Not easy to get weapons these days. Ukraine and Russia are buying up all they can for their war, and they're inflating the price.

"To buy arms at a reasonable price from the Russians, the Mexican government is including tracts of coastal land in their deals as incentives. They're allowing Russians to build military bases there. The Russian government is preparing to establish headquarters on the Mayan coast for their illegal . . ."

Hildie stopped reading to interject her commentary. "And yet, a lot of territory still belongs to local Mexican tribes. This land can't be deeded to anyone who does not belong to a tribe. Something strange is going on if this land is being sold to Russians, and at a cheap price."

Hildie continued reading, "Mexico and Russia are close business partners, with Russia supplying Mexico with fertilizer. Last year, there was an increase of 20% in the fertilizer trade, with over a billion dollars in six months."

Hildie stopped reading to add what she knew. "This is not true. The actual trade includes weapons, not only agriculture. Russian weapons have been found hidden inside bags of fertilizer.

"Since the Ukrainian War," she commented, "Mexico has become a nest for Russian oligarchs. They dock their yachts at their beachfront estates and do business from their yachts. They trade in spying machines and weapons."

I heard the word spying, and became even more interested. Hildie felt my curiosity and commented, "An article from the French *Le Monde* states that currently, Mexico hosts the largest number of Russian spies in the world."

Then she lowered her voice. "I've figured out what they're doing. From Mexico, the Russians use their yachts to go to Florida. They spy on us, and at the same time, they deal in weapons, drugs, and human trafficking.

"From Florida, they sail on to Cuba, not far away, where they've created a Russian vacation spot in Havana with new apartments, even supermarkets filled with Russian food and vodka.

"They're buying up these apartments that are cheap—so from Cuba, they can get to South America by boat and deal in illegal migrant trafficking. The Russians have created a circle of crime and spying—from Mexico to Florida to Cuba to South America and back to Mexico and then on to Florida and the States."

Hildie was getting flushed in the face with her theories. She continued explaining to me: "Recently, Canadian intelligence has reported that there are Russian warships as well as nuclear-powered submarines. These vessels are standing guard at the port of Havana."

Hildie paused and then commented, "Canada must know about this through Mexico's and Russia's spyware."

"What do you mean?"

"Pegasus. Legally, no country is allowed to have access to this spyware. There has been an international accord not to use it. And yet Mexico and Russia still use it."

I remembered how in New York, Laryssa had abruptly taken my cell phone as I was calling home, to see if I was being traced. She had whispered something about Pegasus. She was concerned that someone was tracking me and then through me, following her.

Laryssa had explained to me that military governments have been using Pegasus to spy on dissidents, track them down, and kill them. She appeared to know what she was talking about. She was very concerned.

Hildie excused herself for a moment and said she'd be right back. She wanted to speak to her gardener who was clearing their beach of seaweed.

I stayed alone—thinking and wondering if Alexey was involved with these Russian thugs. They obviously wanted revenge. I was also concerned for Laryssa. Does she know what this is all about? Was she in danger? She did know a lot about their spyware. And Alexey was worried about her, also.

I realized that it would be better for me to stop asking such questions—questions for which I had no answers. Certainly, not yet.

First, I should do what I had set out to do and email Laryssa. I decided not to say anything about Alexey in my message, for fear she might refuse my invitation. I didn't know how she'd react. Instead, I sent her a low-key text: "Hi Laryssa. Hope you're enjoying your stay in Cancun as much as we are in Tulum. We'd love to invite you for lunch if you have some free time. I can send my brother's driver to make it easier."

She quickly responded: "Hi. I'm finding Cancun amazing. Weather is great. Lots of swimming. My husband has to go to Mexico City on business for several days starting tomorrow, something about a military meeting. The Mexican government is sending their plane for him, so I have our driver and would love to visit you. I can be there tomorrow at noon. Please send me your address. I hope you don't mind if I come without my husband. I welcome some time just to be alone."

I decided not to say anything to Alexey. I reasoned that Laryssa might change her mind at the last minute, and I didn't want to disappoint him. I could always tell him tomorrow morning. Or better yet, keep it a surprise.

I also couldn't ignore her response that her husband was involved with the Mexican military, most likely pro-Russian, which meant anti-American.

CHAPTER 17

Miracles do Happen

Alexey had just returned from a morning swim. He was standing in his driveway, emptying his jeep of snorkeling gear. The sun was already strong. He leaned down to the jeep's back seat and took a towel to drape over his neck.

When he picked up his head, he saw a black limo stop beside him. The driver rolled down his window. Alexey moved closer; he rubbed his nose, smelling something mysterious from the back seat.

He looked inside the car. Smelling a sweet perfume, he tried to see who was in the back seat, but there was a black screen blocking his view.

The driver asked him if he knew where Mr. James Kane lived. Alexey pointed to the house to the right of his. The driver thanked him and quickly moved toward the next driveway.

Alexey studied the rear license plate of blue and white with the letters DPL, which he recognized as diplomat. A common sight for him in Washington, but here, on his private, dusty road in Mexico? He wondered who the diplomat could be, visiting James. How strange, he thought. And the perfume. It reminded him of something from a long time ago. Sweet like roses. He breathed in deeply, closed his eyes, and tried to remember.

He took his snorkeling gear into the house, went to the kitchen for a glass of water, and peered out his window towards his neighbor's beach. James and Hildie were not there, but Sybil was. She was dressed in a bathing suit with a beach towel wrapped around her shoulders. She had been swimming.

Sitting next to her was a woman, wearing a light blue sun dress. The two were talking and laughing, but he could only see their backs, both bare in the sun. Sybil stood up to go inside the house, pointing to her bathing suit, indicating to the woman that she wanted to change into clothes.

Alexey studied the woman who was left alone. Her face was covered by a large, brimmed straw hat. She was wearing dark sunglasses. But suddenly, she took off her hat, put her fingers through her hair, and Alexey saw the full red curls.

It was Laryssa! He was sure it was her. It could be no one else! He remembered Sybil said she knew her. They were friends. She'd said she would contact her. But Sybil had left it at that, with no further details or follow up. And now, Laryssa had appeared before him, like magic, and she was all alone.

Alexey felt a sensation of panic. How would he proceed? What should he do?

He took a T-shirt from his front closet, decided to stay in his bathing shorts so as not to waste time, and walked toward the beach where she was sitting. His instinct was to move closer to her, approach her quietly, humbly, show himself in all his bareness, like a beggar, without signs of money or success. Bare, with only his love.

But he paused and closed his eyes to gather strength. He took a deep breath. How would he begin? What would he say?

He felt afraid and stood behind a palm tree. He waited. He thought. He listened. He tried to breathe in the perfume of the beautiful lady with the golden shoulders. He remembered his small student room that smelled like a garden of roses. He remembered their making love for the first time. After nights together, his room had absorbed her presence, taken her scent, made the walls sweet, creating for him a Garden of Eden.

His mouth was dry. There was a gnawing sensation in his stomach. He tried to calm himself by taking deep breaths. He leaned harder against the tree, rubbed his back and sunburned shoulders against the rough bark to feel the pain. He needed to strengthen himself.

Laryssa, what are you doing here? In all his dreams, he had never thought he would see her again.

She stood up to put her purse on the table, taking several steps to stare at the sea. He remembered that she walked like she was dancing, with a rhythm in her body for which only she knew the tune.

He became fixated on her hair, the same fiery red flames beneath the large straw hat. He couldn't see her face.

Unexpectedly, a sudden burst of sunlight bathed the beach where she was standing, and she turned her face to the side. He saw her cheek, chiseled and set high above her oval face and strong chin. She moved away from the sun, blinking her eyes, a furtive blue, reflecting the sea before her.

He wanted to walk over to her, but his legs wouldn't move. He willed his body to push forward, but his legs stiffened; they felt heavy, rigid.

He closed his eyes to pray that love was stronger than time.

Who was this woman, now, thirty-two years later?

Slowly, his courage returned, and he willed himself forward.

Laryssa leaned against the table to adjust her hat. She reached to free her hair, shook her curls in the wind, and then turned her head. She saw him and stopped. She couldn't move, frozen in confusion, not knowing what to do. Was it Alexey? Was it truly him or someone who looked like him? What was he doing here? Could this be possible?

Alexey moved towards her slowly.

Everything around her stopped.

She felt her body shiver as if the hard shell holding it together had cracked. She looked down at the ground, searching for the pieces. Who could she blame for thirty years lost? Time gone forever. It was the fault of circumstances that their love had not been shared.

He ran towards her, taking her into his arms, covering her tears with kisses. He held her in his arms and there they stayed together, hardly breathing, afraid to move.

Time had stopped.

* * *

Alexey listened to Laryssa breathe, his cheek on her breast. It reminded him of how he had held her after they had made love, so many years ago. He'd tried to breathe with her, match the same rhythm of her heart, become one with her.

They sat down on the sand. He took her hand to his lips and softly kissed each finger. She put her head in his lap and wept. "Please forgive me. I'm so sorry.

"Let me first explain why I didn't follow you," she said, "and then we'll talk of other things."

He caressed the fine lines under her eyes, shadows of gray. They spoke of sorrow.

"The morning after you told me you were leaving Minsk with your father, I told my mother that I was going to marry you and leave with you for the States.

"She cried and cried; my father sobbed. And then, within minutes, she fell to the ground, unconscious. We couldn't wake her. My father called an ambulance, and they took her to the hospital. After several hours, the doctors were able to resuscitate her, but she couldn't move her right side; her right arm and leg were rigid. The right side of her face was motionless. The doctor said it was a stroke. It could take months for her to recover, if she ever did.

"You had told me you needed my answer in a few days. I was ashamed to tell you what had happened to my mother. I blamed myself. I prayed and prayed she'd get better quickly so I could join you. I wanted a miracle . . ." She paused, breathing harder. "There was no miracle.

"I had to tell you no. My guilt prevented me from telling you the truth. I wanted so much to leave with you but how could I? Leave my father alone with my mother? Leave my mother alone when she had a stroke because of me?

"I felt like a criminal—taking life from my mother who I loved so much. I couldn't leave her, and I couldn't tell you that I had harmed my mother. The truth was shameful to me."

Alexey took Laryssa in his arms. What could he answer her? How could he blame her for doing what was right? And yet, he had never known the truth. He had had to live his life without her. He closed his eyes.

She put her head against his heart and she, too, cried.

"There's so much I want to ask you," he said. "So much to tell you. Can we walk on the beach and talk?"

She stood up, he took her hand. "I, too, am not free of blame. I should have insisted on finding out the truth. And I should have waited for you, helped you." He looked down, ashamed. "I didn't. Yet, I know now, that if I would have returned to Minsk from the States to get you, they would have killed me. You too."

"Please don't blame yourself," she said, putting her arm through his as they walked. "You didn't know. I kept the truth from you. And that was unfair. I didn't give you the chance to choose what to do. But I did that intentionally—I didn't want you to lose the chance to leave. You couldn't have stayed in that hell when you had an opportunity to be free."

"I didn't know . . ." he kept mumbling. His anguish kept increasing. "For now, I only want to know one thing—do you still love me?"

She took his hand and placed it on her heart. "Alexey, I swear before God, I never stopped loving you. And I will always love you. No matter what happens."

He stared hard at her and picked her up in his arms. "That's all I want to know. Let me take you to my home."

She laughed. "Put me down. You'll hurt yourself." They both laughed as he carried her away.

She didn't have time to look where she was going. He took her through his house, all the time carrying her as if he were afraid he'd lose her again.

"I've waited so long. I've missed you so much." He placed her in his bed, kissing her as he took off each article of her clothing. She did the same to him, slowly at first, laughing and teasing and then with a deep rush.

"I've been wanting to save you—from all the evil in this world," he said, kissing her.

"And only you can save me."

They stopped laughing. He took her in his arms and held her, kissing her neck, her cheeks, her lips. Time had disappeared. They were together.

Slowly, he finished removing all of her clothes. He kissed her breasts, her stomach, her full passionate lips that whispered more. She unbuttoned his shirt, his pants. She stroked his body with her hands, her lips. She moved closer, tighter, wanting more and more. The heat of passion burned inside. She was on fire. He pressed his lips against the pulsating veins of her neck. He took each breast in his palm and kissed her nipples until they were hard. He moved into her, entered deep with all his hunger. She lost herself in him. Her passion raised her higher and higher, deeper and deeper. She floated up, wanting to burst. Scream. Yell. Die.

There was no place, no time, no memory at all. Only their joy in being together.

He kissed her wet hair, soft and damp with desire. He drank in her passion as she moved beneath him. Their bodies burned as one and in their fire, they forgot where they were, where they were going.

There was no stopping, no waiting. Two lovers resurrected, making up for so many years without each other.

CHAPTER 18

Time Stops for Love; Laryssa's Confessions

"I don't feel like getting out of bed." Alexey said, kissing Laryssa.

"Me neither," she cuddled into his arms.

"Do you love me? Really love me?" he whispered in her ear.

"I've never loved anyone but you."

"And your husband? Niklaus Nikolai, the General? What are your feelings for him?"

She waved her hand as if she were waving him away. "Nikky has been a vehicle. Let me explain the real reason we're together: my work.

"First, I must confess to you, although I have sworn secrecy . . . I want you to know that I've been working with Vlad and the underground since you left for the States. You know the rules for disclosure, my pledge to the CIA."

He nodded. "I swear myself to secrecy."

She hesitated to find the right words. "I want to confess to you my involvement with the Resistance, so you'll trust me. That's very important."

He took her hand to encourage her to speak.

"I had nothing left inside me when you left," she told him. "It was as if I had a hole inside me. Loosing you made me feel hollow. In order to survive, I realized I would have to fill the hole."

Alexey took both her hands. She looked down.

"I returned often to our bistro. I lived in my memory."

He closed his eyes.

"I thought if I could become active in the resistance with Vlad Makei, I could feel useful, have important work to keep me alive, and above all, I could pretend we're working together.

"I contacted Vlad, our dear friend, who swore to me he'd never tell you. And he'd find a way that I could help. I was already working in the ministry."

"He never told me," Alexey said. "But I must say, sometimes the thought crossed my mind. The three of us were so close, emotionally and politically.

"So, what did you do for the cause?" he asked her, teasingly. "Use your beauty or your brains?"

She pretended to bite him. "You're too inquisitive, my love. Let me confess, slowly, so you'll trust me," she laughed.

Then she answered, seriously: "Vlad recruited me as a spy. To work for the Americans."

She took a deep breath, continued.

"He arranged for me to be trained for three months in Sibiu, Romania, where the CIA has a cell for intelligence agents from Eastern Europe. It was a type of espionage school where I learned how to protect myself physically, mentally, and psychologically.

"The CIA was particularly interested in my dissertation on conflict resolution and wanted me to learn more about the subject. I actually took courses with a senior operative about the topic from a military and judicial perspective."

"That's interesting. They must have had a plan in mind to use you and your knowledge."

"I believe so. They encouraged me to write a treatise about strategy for Belarus and Russia by using conflict resolution in time of war."

"I see they found your talent—putting strategies together to solve the problems of mutinies and dissent."

"Yes. And that remains my focus, even today. Mostly mutinies. What the West should do if there's a potential uprising." She smiled at him.

He nodded, wondering what she was leading to. Did she foresee something would happen in Russia? A mutiny? A coup d'état in Belarus?

She continued. "There were five other women in my group, but we trained separately, each one alone with one CIA operative.

"I worked with Charles—or at least he said his name was Charles. He was a specialist in military strategy. He taught me about explosives, firearms, and tanks. How to build a trench, hide in it, and reappear to throw hand grenades. I also learned from him the digital aspects of several countries' cyber security systems—how to send codes and take videos. How to get into their cyber world.

"I enjoyed that the most. It was like a chess game. In my mind, I set up the chess board with two opponents—me and Russia. I had to find their weaknesses and strategize when to attack by air, sea, or land. I realized that this war will depend on cyber activity—drones and radar. I had to use digital as well as technical knowledge.

"But I also enjoyed hand-to-hand combat." She smiled. "Strange for a woman, yes?"

Alexey nodded. "I did notice how muscular you've become but I was afraid to comment. You'd be a match for me."

She kissed him. "My secret. Yes, my instructor said I was strong, with innate timing. These skills also helped me at the shooting range."

"The best timing you had was to come to Mexico." Alexey's smile turned serious. "I imagine that was not accidental."

She smiled. "There are no coincidences. Destiny. Fate. A miracle."

"I guess you're good at opening locks, vaults, safes, hearts?" He tried to smile. "Lots of hearts?" he asked. "Charles'?"

"Alexey, you sound jealous," she counter-attacked, trying to avoid responding.

"My dear Laryssa, you have become a very dangerous woman."

She smiled, rather pleased, taking his words as a compliment.

"The next thing our friend Vlad did for me," she confessed, "was to organize with the Ukrainian army's cyber division. Alina and I would set up a cell of spymasters among our chess colleagues who were anti-Russian. Alina was in Kyiv, and she worked with the Ukrainians involved in the cyber operation. I was in Minsk and coordinated the details from my side. That's where my training in cyber security from Romania proved invaluable."

"I didn't know about your chess operation."

"No, it was all secret. Those were the rules."

He nodded in understanding, but was still puzzled.

"The next thing Vlad did for me was to arrange this fake marriage with the general. My assets had been frozen because of sanctions. And I wasn't allowed to travel. Vlad's plan was for me to marry a diplomat affiliated with the UN—either that or a general. In either case, I could use a diplomatic passport as a spouse.

"In this way, I could get to Minsk to report to Vlad personally what I was learning while in New York, and from Minsk, safely back to New York to continue.

"Nikky was part of this plan. He was a chess pawn in our group. He'd include me in his work at the UN, as well as make information available to me from his dealings in Washington. I became the donkey, going back and forth to Minsk with everything memorized."

Alexey made a grimace. "Very risky for you. I wonder if Vlad made a mistake with this scheme."

Then he paused, didn't finish his thought. Instead, he asked her: "So, tell me, did you sleep with your general? Or did you just have a meeting of the minds?"

"No! The answer is no. It was a marriage of convenience. That was the deal. Vlad had assured Nikky that once democracy was voted in, he'd see that the general would get what he wanted as his reward. Nikky has a big ego. He wants to become minister of defense or chief of the military for Belarus."

"He accepted this deal? This charade? I find it hard to believe that he resisted your beauty."

Alexey paced his room.

"Do you have separate bedrooms?"

"Yes."

"He's never tried to come close to you. Knock on your door at night?"

She didn't want to tell him that last month, the general had come home late after drinking and playing cards with friends. He had lost a fortune. He was in a rage, and drunk . . .

> *"Let me in!" he'd yelled at her while banging on her door. "Let me in!"*
> *She had run from her bed into the bathroom, but before she could lock the door, he was already next to her, kicking her with his foot.*
> *She took a large bottle of perfume and smashed the bottle at his feet.*
> *He slapped her. "Take off your nightgown!"*
> *"No!"*
> *He pushed her against the wall, kicking her, banging her head against the door.*
> *She fell down on the tiled floor.*
> *"You're not the only woman in this city!" he said, slamming the door. He left her, sobbing, bleeding.*

"What are you thinking?" Alexey said, taking her hand.

She showed him her thumb, scarred and disfigured. "This is Nikky's doing. I tell my friends it's from fixing my house and using a hammer, but it was Nikky's violence."

Alexey took her in his arms. "My poor Laryssa. I don't trust your general at all."

Alexey went to his closet, opened a secret compartment, took out a small machine and spoke into it. After several seconds, he whispered to her, "I've assigned my assistant to find out a little more about your fake husband. He should be punished!"

Alexey paced his room again, trying to calm himself. He took Laryssa in his arms and stroked her hair.

"Sometimes he had me followed," she confessed. "I'd recognize the security guard from the Mission tailing me in the street. I'd run away, try to lose him. I'd enter a store, go to their bathroom, and wait a while before going back into the street. But once, when I was having coffee with Sybil, the guard was waiting for me as I was leaving the cafe.

"He grabbed my arm, pushed me into the Mission's car. I kicked him, trying to get free. I tried to open the car door and jump out. But it was impossible. He was twice my size.

"When we arrived at the Mission, he pulled me to Nikky's office. 'Here she is!' he reported, practically throwing my body to him.

"Nikky slapped me. 'Why were you away so long? Who are you talking to?'"

"At that moment, I realized things between us had turned dark. I couldn't take it anymore. This was only last week, before coming to Mexico."

Alexey held her in his arms, softly, tenderly. "I'm trying to think why Vlad put you into such a terrible situation. He must have had a reason."

Then in a more controlled voice, Alexey asked her, "Did the general ever do anything beneficial for you? Did you gain anything by being with him?"

"There is something he does for me," she said, pensively. "He takes me to his meetings at the Pentagon as his deputy, something he officially arranged with the proper ID, being that I was part of the Ministry. I think his ulterior motive was to keep me near."

"I agree," Alexey commented. "Keep your friends close and your enemies closer."

"Once we're inside, he takes me to the private dining room and arranges a time to meet me. But I don't stay there. He goes to his contacts, and I go to mine—without him knowing. I wish I could tell you who his contacts are."

Alexey returned to his closet and machine, whispered something that Laryssa couldn't hear.

She walked over to the window and examined her thumb. "Nikky has been useful to our cause," she said, but in a hesitant voice.

Alexey's suspicions had reinforced her doubts about Nikky. Lately, she had reason not to trust him. And it seemed as if they didn't trust each other. With Vlad no longer alive to monitor Nikky, he was doing what he wanted. And it wasn't in Laryssa's interest. She wondered who he reports to.

Alexey paced the room. "Laryssa, I did not know about your espionage training. I didn't know about your fake husband or your work with him at the UN. Vlad had never shared this information with me. Why, I don't know.

"And I wonder how thoroughly Vlad had your general vetted. Did Vlad look away so you could have entry into the Pentagon and work with your contacts without Nikky or anyone else knowing? Was that Vlad's objective? Did he put you into a difficult situation on purpose? Watch how you'd react? Where you'd turn?

"Human nature is so unpredictable. Everyone turns to the one who gives him the most. Vlad shouldn't have tempted you by putting you in danger."

"What are you talking about?" She didn't like the turn of his thinking.

"Nothing."

He paused, took a deep breath, and then continued.

"I'm now a senior operative, very senior, and still I've been unaware of the details of your espionage involvement. And listening to you speak of Nikky makes me highly suspicious of him. I'm waiting to get some proof to back up my suspicions.

"I also find it odd that the Americans kept you secret from me. As you're telling me how you were recruited, what your work is, and your fake marriage, I'm wondering why the CIA kept me out of the loop about you?"

"I think," she commented, "that they must be aware of our involvement together when we were students. The CIA does not approve of emotional attachments between operatives."

"Yes," he agreed. "A situation could arise when the enemy would try to break me because of you. I would have talked to save you." A potential problem, he realized.

"Tell me, apart from the activities you've just described to me, what were the details of Vlad's recruiting you. And what was, or is, your personal mission with the CIA? As well as your work with Nikky."

She hesitated. "Let's go outside to the beach. I have an aversion to walls with ears."

Before they left the room, Alexey touched all the walls for microphones, tapes or digital chips. "I believe what we've said is confidential."

"And your pillow?" she added, eyeing his bed. "Pillow talk is always interesting to a spying, peeping Tom."

"He'd blush, watching our passion."

* * *

They chatted in a whisper as they strolled the beach, talking of this and that. They were alone and no one could hear. When she finished speaking of her work, Alexey quoted T. S. Eliot and "The Love Song of J. Alfred Prufrock":

> *"Let us go then you and I, when the day is spread out against the sky . . . to lead you to an overwhelming question . . . Oh, do not ask, what is it? Let us go and make our visit . . ."*

"Have you enjoyed being a spy?" Alexey asked her.

She laughed.

He replied for her: "I always thought you'd make a good spy: daring, courageous, secretive."

"Is that a compliment or insult?"

"One of the few enigmas of your character. You have many. One fights the other. I remember a Cherokee parable that fits your character perfectly," he commented:

> *"There are two wolves inside each person. When asked which wolf wins, an elder replies, 'Whichever one you feed.'"*

She looked at him, long and hard, and moved away.

He realized that he had discovered the conflict of her soul. He knew he'd have to remember this about her despite loving her so much.

"Actually, I did find being a spy . . . instructive," she commented. "I learned a lot about survival."

"Survival is not always moral. Tell me."

"One: how to implement psychological manipulation to extract information from an individual.

"Two: every human being is a puzzle of needs. To get what you want, find the person's needs.

"And three: it becomes hard to satisfy ambition."

Alexey walked away. Then he turned towards her but said nothing.

She continued talking, trying to negate his doubts about her.

"My leader gave me the greatest compliment at the end of my training," Laryssa commented. He told me, 'Your talent is to be one step ahead of anyone else's scheming.'"

Alexey picked up a rock and threw it to the sea. "Tell me," he asked her, "how did Vlad test you to determine if you'd make a capable spy? To survive by any means?"

"I was to travel from Minsk to Cluj in Romania, all alone, by using only my guile."

Alexey nodded. "That you have!"

"I put it to work." And she recounted how:

"I had to take the train from Minsk through Kyiv, south to Bucharest, during a violent uprising in Romania after communism. A bloody time there.

"The CIA gave me very little money and just some bread and cheese. They provided me with a fake ID that I hid, but there was no guarantee it would work. What helped me was that I decided to dress up as a boy—a boy selling newspapers. I found such a boy—sleeping in the station."

She didn't explain how she got his wares. Or how she dared to dress the role.

"I went through the trains, striding like a boy, speaking in a deep voice, carrying a large backpack full of newspapers. *'Zviazda! Novaya Gazeta! Kommersant! Pravda!'*"

"I spoke in Russian as I went southbound to Ukraine, and English when in Romania." She demonstrated for Alexey her body movements, pretending she was a boy, carrying a heavy load on her back, and yelling to sell her goods.

Caught up in her story, he pretended he was one of her customers, trying to flirt with her, touching her breasts. She slapped his hand and they both laughed. "I'm supposed to be a boy!"

"Oh, I forgot."

And she continued her narration.

"I was a boy by day, selling my goods, but the trip was two days long with one overnight. I had to sleep."

"That's true." He reviewed the distance in his mind: 1200 kilometers from Belarus to Transylvania. "So, what did you do?"

"I found lodging in another car of the train. I roomed with the cows."

Alexey laughed. Despite her story being hazardous, he admired her guile.

"I climbed into the last car of the train. It was full of cattle. As I moved through the hay, I saw two cows who mooed. I feared they'd give me away.

"'Shh . . . shh,' I whispered and patted them as if they were friends. I gave them some straw from the floor, which they accepted as a bribe. I think they didn't realize I was a person at all. I smelled like the other cows in the stall.

"As I was searching for a safe spot to sleep, I noticed in the wooden wall of the car, a small round hole for air, the same size as my eye. When the train moved, I placed one eye against the hole to watch the hills and mountains pass by.

"In my imagination, the round opening became a kaleidoscope, and I could watch the mosaic colors of Belarus and Ukraine.

"As the sun began to set, I saw streaks of red and orange. I stared at the sun as it colored the snow on the mountains red. It looked as if the sky was splintering into a thousand fires. No painter could have brushed the red so passionately on a blue sky.

"I was fixated on the small opening as the day was ending. Crimson colors shadowed green pine trees in between mountain cliffs; colors from blue rivers flowed into white waterfalls. It was as if I was viewing nature through tinted lenses.

"I put my ear to the hole to hear the calm. Only the timbre of cow bells going home echoed throughout.

"I knew I was experiencing something mystical. It reminded me of times with you. When we would hike in the mountains together and lodge in a small cabin. Once, I got up early from your arms and left you sleeping. I ran through the cold room to where there was a fireplace. I wanted to surprise you by making hot tea.

"I remember watching the soft mist of morning color our window in crimson while I prepared logs in the fireplace. Smoke outside the window, appeared pink from the morning sun. The entire cabin was colored red by the blazing fire. I looked outside and saw the grass was covered in a morning blanket of pink and white frost. I thought of how much I loved you and how I wanted you to start your day happy.

"These are the memories I kept to fill my hollow heart when I was left without you. They were the scenes that I held tight in my soul as I became a spy to be close to you. It was from loving you that I had confidence I could create a new life for myself.

"I remember you once said to me, 'Whenever life seems the lowest, that's when you must rise. Use your willpower to survive.'"

CHAPTER 19

Demonstration and Intimidation in the Mexican Pueblo; Laryssa's Mission

Alexey was awakened from his morning sleep by loud noises, people yelling in the pueblo, and babies crying. He went to the terrace to assess the commotion when a rock hit his chest, then another rock struck his arm.

He saw three men, with shaven heads, dressed in Russian army uniforms. Each one was carrying in one hand a heavy bicycle chain and in the other a torch with flames at its tip. They were marching on the dirt road leading to his house. Above them, flying low, was a helicopter. Alexey was able to see the red, blue and white Russian flag painted on its door. He realized the helicopter, slightly ahead of the men, was guiding them to his house.

People at the side of the road were throwing rocks and sticks at the three men.

Alexey ran inside and into his bedroom to check on Laryssa's safety. She hadn't heard the altercation since was in the bathroom taking a shower.

"Get dressed, quickly!" he shouted to her, opening the shower door.

He went to his closet and sent a coded message to ask for backup. Then he went to his bureau and took out two machine guns. He threw one to Laryssa as she was getting dressed and told her, "Three Russians want our attention."

Laryssa caught the gun and ran to the terrace with Alexey. They bent down on their knees, periodically looking up through the closed window.

Several Mexican gardeners had left their construction work and were using their steel shovels to strike the three men in uniform. The Russians, retaliated by flicking their steel chains at them and taunted them with their torches. One Russian had a machine gun and shot the ground at the Mexicans' feet.

Laryssa and Alexey saw a young Mexican boy run into the middle of the dirt road and throw rocks at the hoodlums who were swinging their chains at him. The boy darted into a building, and a second later, he ran out, holding a pistol and shooting into the air.

Chaos took over. Gunfire. Sirens. The Mexican police blasted their car loudspeaker and stormed their jeep toward the three Russians.

Laryssa saw a woman run out of a store carrying a baby. Laryssa yelled at her through the window, "*Cuidado! Vaya a casa!* Go home!" The woman ran behind a shed.

One of the Russians saw Laryssa yell and took aim at her. Alexey attached a belt of ammunition on to his rifle and began shooting a dozen bullets per second. Laryssa backed him up and together, they quickly shot the three men dead within seconds.

The helicopter following the men took another direction away from the chaos. Fire engines and police cars entered the dirt road and stopped in front of the three dead bodies.

Alexey said to Laryssa, "I'll speak to the police. You stay inside."

He went into the street, took out a card, flashed it in front of the chief and patted him on his back. "*Amigo* . . ." Alexey began, and his remaining words were lost in the crowd.

After a couple of minutes, Alexey put several dollar bills into the policeman's pocket and walked away. The chief of police addressed the crowd, "*Vaya a su casa.* Go home," and slowly, the people left the site. Laryssa opened her window and surveyed the bloody road.

Several policemen dispersed the mob and covered the bodies with blankets. For the police, it was no different than a drug war, and they treated the bloody road as they always did. They took out a bag from the trunk of their car and covered the red road with brown sand.

The gardeners returned to their work. People came out into the street and chattered in a frenzy with a new topic to discuss. Vendors opened their stores and addressed their customers with gossip of the moment.

Life in the Mexican pueblo continued as before.

* * *

Alexey handed Laryssa a cup of coffee. "Are you ok?" he asked her.

"Yes, please don't worry about me."

"I'm afraid these are not the last of our visitors."

"Is this the first time that this has happened?"

"Not as close—a previous quarrel in a restaurant, a car chase, even a boat harassment. Russians working with the Mexican government who give them free rein to cause trouble. I've received word from my operatives that they're part of the FSB, the old KGB. They're linked to the Mexican military, trying to intimidate me."

"Why?"

"Someone must know who I am. I've been exposed, compromised. And I think I know who has done it."

"Who?" she was worried for him.

The leader's name is Boris Antonovich. Do you know him?

"No."

"You should. I've been told he's the cousin of your general."

"Nikky?"

"You have another general?" He smiled at her.

"I don't know this Boris," she answered.

"He's a thug. I wouldn't be surprised if he and your general share more than just a blood line. Boris is an enemy, and it makes me like Nikky even less."

"Please share with me any feedback you get from your inquiries," she asked, concerned that Nikky may know where she is. "I wish I never got involved with this Nikky," she whispered under her breath.

She sighed, bit her lip, and suggested to Alexey, "Perhaps this is the moment for you to get backup. A couple of security guards you can trust. Or operatives."

"Yes, I've sent a request to Washington. Especially, that we're two here, working for the same group."

"That'll be practical." she said, trying to reassure him. "Alexey, don't worry about me. I'm not afraid. And Nikky? I must confess, I've had doubts about him. But it's best for you to find out from objective sources what's his game rather than it coming from me."

"I'll find out about both cousins." He looked at her reassuringly. "And now, more important, tell me what would you like for breakfast? Do you still love fruit and buttered toast?"

"Yes," she smiled, "and I love you."

He kissed her. "I still can't believe you're here."

She stood up and hugged him.

"What would you like to do after breakfast?" he asked her in a softer tone. "Go swimming? Visit the center of town? It's calm now."

"I just want to be with you."

* * *

They took a walk to the beach and strolled through the dunes. The sun was just beginning to rise. Red and orange colors streaked the sky. Birds chirped as they rested on bushes. The tide was high, and waves swept softly against the jetty rocks. A rhythm of calm overwhelmed them.

"It's so beautiful here," she said, studying the waves. She kissed him. "I love you so much, Alexey."

"And I love you, my beautiful, *intrigante* spy."

She laughed. "I think I'm surprising you."

"Nothing you do surprises me." He laughed. "You are a mystery through and through. I'll never know what to expect from you."

"You won't get bored."

"Never."

"Then let me tell you more."

"I'm all ears."

"You asked me about my mission with the CIA. The truth, my love, is that I was recruited to report on one big fish—the whale—Lukashenko."

"Wow! The catch of the day! Your CIA friends must have a lot of confidence in you. Vlad handed you a heavy weight to bring in and he never told me about it."

"I'm well connected," she teased him, laughing. "Better be nice to me," and then she turned serious.

"My relationship with Lukashenko has been invaluable to the CIA. Also to the State Department. My orders are to stay close to Lukashenko. To have his trust and give him advice—advice that he listens to. That's my primary mission. I, in turn, report to senior operatives in a different unit than yours."

She hesitated. "Alexey, I love you. You have to trust me. What I'm going to tell you is all true and top secret. I shouldn't be telling you this."

"I swear." He raised his hand as a promise. "Only you and I can trust each other. Remember that. Do not trust anyone else, but me, from now on."

"I know." She took his hand and put it to her lips. "That has been the hardest thing for me—to always remember, I cannot trust someone. To be closed with others." She looked down and took a deep breath. "Now I have you."

She smiled and continued.

"My assignment is in two phases. The first phase was after my training in Romania. When I finished, I applied for a low-level position in Belarus's ministry, working with the media division and press. Vlad helped me from the beginning to move up the ladder. My work was to first become indispensable to Lukashenko regarding press coverage. He used my reports for TV and media. And I used his confidence to find out everything I could pass on to my group of operatives.

"It was important for my colleagues to have a full profile of Lukashenko. To know who was visiting him in Minsk, as well as where he was traveling, and who he was meeting. I even arranged specific locations for his schedule to facilitate things so that my CIA backup could follow him."

"You reported all your findings each day on a special code-machine?"

"Yes, like you do from your closet." She winked at him—her fellow spy.

"What I did today was to investigate Nikky, not you," Alexey said defensively, pointing his finger at her as if he were scolding her. "Tell me," he said, "you were tapped to stay close to Lukashenko? How close were you both?"

"I resent that question," she said calmly but with a tinge of irritation. "And I resent even more your suspicions."

"Lukashenko is a womanizer. Everyone knows that. The beautiful women who've worked for him have found his bed and favors." Alexey gave her a sarcastic grin. He was trying to control his demeanor. "Hard to give up a powerful man, if you don't have to give him up."

"What are you implying?"

"It's the press that's implying."

"Be careful, Alexey" she said, now becoming hurt. "You can't lose trust in me because you're jealous."

But Alexey wasn't finished with his inquisition.

"Tell me, do you still hike in Switzerland? Still have your ski chalet in Davos?"

"Yes, I do."

"I hear you also have a farmhouse outside Minsk. And there's your apartment in the center of the city. All from your modest salary? No perks?"

"Have you been checking up on me? Did you also get access to my bank account?"

Alexey looked down. "Yes, I did."

"How dare you!" Laryssa lost her temper.

"It's on record that you are one of the richest female politicians in Belarus. Valued at ten million plus. I need to be sure I can trust you, Laryssa. Please explain how you've accumulated so much wealth."

She hesitated, insulted, but she knew she needed to explain. She'd tell him the truth. "My first husband, the father of my daughters, came from a well-connected family. They had a large estate and farm, because they had ties to the party. He was their only child. When he died, I inherited it all, and then later, I sold it. I was concerned about finances. I was alone with the girls, and I'd need to educate them properly."

She looked down, hurt that he had requested the information from her in such a cold manner. And that he had gathered the proofs so quickly without her knowing.

"Please forgive me, Laryssa. Remember that I love you and I must be sure I'm right in loving you."

"I understand," she said, suppressing her anger. She knew that for both of them it was hard to trust others. That was the residual damage of being a spy.

"Let's go on," she said in a more controlled manner. "Let me continue explaining my work. Phase two of my recruitment was at the United Nations. My task is to document every foreign country that votes with Belarus and Russia and what the general's involvement is to bring these votes forward. That is essential to determine who the Americans can trust or not. In addition, I catalogue who Nikky meets in Washington. That has been the most difficult responsibility for me because we go our separate ways to meetings. I to my contacts, and he to his. I'm still not able to pinpoint his associates. It's been very frustrating for me."

"High risk, again."

Alexey stood up and started to pace the beach. Returning to his chair next to her, he asked her about Nikky. Alexey seemed to be fixated on her relations with men.

"He must know what you do, whom you meet, what you scheme? Even your secret relationships with senior officials?"

"I'm not sure about that."

Alexey took her hand. "My beautiful *intrigante*, what else have you been doing? You've been very busy."

She nodded yes and ignored his sarcasm. "You know that Romania has been nominated by NATO and the European Union to lead an investigation and to gather proof related to the Ukrainian children who've been abducted and relocated to Russian and Belarusian territory.

"It seems that the Belarusian Red Cross is responsible for transporting kidnapped children across borders. Forcible abduction is a crime. And yet, the Red Cross headquarters in Geneva claims that they know nothing about it. How can this be true?"

"It reminds me how the International Red Cross worked with Nazi war criminals after the war to get them new passports and identity, even money, and helped transport them to South America to hide."

She knew that many of these fascists died in their warm beds and were never punished. "You should have the Red Cross investigated, rather than me," she commented.

He nodded his head and looked down, ashamed.

"How is it possible that history repeats itself?" Laryssa asked him. "I know that in Belarus, they've been taking the kidnapped children to a sanatorium near Vitebsk, where your father and Chagall were born, and to Dubrava near the capital, where I have my farmhouse."

Alexey made a grimace. "The evidence is to be used at the International Criminal Court in The Hague in a similar way that they did at Nuremberg against German war criminals."

"Yes. Putin and his Minister of Children, Maria Lvova-Belov, have already been accused of crimes against humanity. I'm working now to gather evidence about Lukashenko's role," she told him. "It seems that he has recruited his entire family to transport kidnapped children to Belarus."

Laryssa paused and took a deep breath. She was angry. "Alexey, I want the Belarusian criminals involved in stealing children to be punished."

She lowered her head. "You asked me what's my personal mission with the CIA—it's to help the Ukrainian children return home."

CHAPTER 20

Mexican Wedding in the Pueblo; Bacchante Dancing

The following day, Alexey announced to Laryssa, "I've been invited to a wedding. My housekeeper, Florita, is getting married to Juanito. She wants me to give her away."

Laryssa smiled. "How lovely."

"It's a custom here, an honor. The boss gives his blessings."

"I'd love to join the party. What fun." Then she hesitated. "But I have nothing to wear."

Alexey laughed. "Did you ever know that I wanted to be a dress designer?"

"What? You? Would you dress your women in army fatigues?"

He laughed. "It's true. I wanted to be a designer. You once told me that you wished you could be a professional singer. You were great with Vlad at the piano. And I too, have an alter ego."

"I would never have thought you had such a creative side."

"Ahh. DNA from my grandfather, the artist. It's beauty I crave—like you." He kissed her. "Let me prove it to you. I will make you a party dress like no other."

"Really?"

"Yes! Give me the chance. But you have to help me."

"My pleasure."

Alexey gave Laryssa several directives: "Do you have any scarves or beach *sarongs*?"

"Yes, I did bring several with me."

"In dramatic colors? Made of silk?"

"Yes."

"Your lovely straw hat?"

"Of course."

"Good. And I have lots of flowers in my garden. Scarves and flowers—that's all I need for material. Most important of all, is your beautiful body."

She laughed. "I can't wait!"

"Festivities begin in two hours," Alexey commented. "I'll wear a white suit and white shirt and you, my dear, will be garnished in flowers and silk. My beautiful model, please collect your fabrics now and I'll gather the flowers. And then, I hope you're willing to strip to your naked, lovely self, so I can begin."

Fifteen minutes later, Laryssa was standing naked in Alexey's bedroom. Laying at her feet were dozens of red, pink, yellow flowers, and scarves of fine silk.

Alexey kissed her stomach, commenting on how he loved her midriff and breasts. "I will keep them exposed in my design. I can't cover the best parts of your body. And I want you to feel free. To be my uninhibited muse."

He began his design by wrapping her in silks of blue, green, yellow, and red. And as promised, he left uncovered most of her breasts and middle torso. He left an opening in the front of her legs with a slit made of panels of red silk. The artist wanted her long, slender legs to be free to dance and show their grace.

He placed dozens of rose buds tucked in her hair, making a crown with a string of daisies at her forehead.

"Magnificent, my love!" he exclaimed. "Your elegance enhances the design. Let me show you."

He took a long mirror and shared with her his vision of beauty.

"Wow! You have an extraordinary talent."

"No, my dear, what is extraordinary is you. You've inspired me." He kissed her and both model and artist stood there like children, laughing.

Alexey parted to dress in his white suit; he even wore a white Mexican hat. Laryssa crowned herself with her large straw hat, now decorated by Alexey with the same rose petals in her red curls and surrounding her breasts.

The main street of the pueblo was filled with waiting guests—all dressed for a fiesta. Alexey and Laryssa joined James, Hildie, Gene and Sybil. Then Alexey kissed Laryssa's hand as he departed and moved to join the bride.

Mexican musicians, dressed in festive suits of embroidered silk and gold, with large brown hats and wide rims, formed a long line parallel to the square's main street. They played on their guitars and accordions a Spanish wedding march as Florita, dressed in white, and Alexey, her escort, walked proudly into the pueblo square.

Guests and neighbors cheered and threw rose petals, yelling joyfully, "*Oya! Oya! Una boda en el pueblo! Què linda!* A beautiful wedding!"

The groom, Juanito, approached them. He waved to the crowd with his large, black sombrero, and then lowered his head to Alexey in respect, and took his bride's hand to kiss it.

The crowd screamed, "*Amor! Amor! Por siempre!*"

The musicians played, "*La Cucaracha. La Cucaracha,*" and children danced in the street. A wedding of love. Everyone in the pueblo was happy.

The bride and groom stood in front of the crowd, smiling and serious, both dressed in their wedding finery. Periodically a photographer would flash a light, and Florita lowered her eyes, pleased. She was perfect in her role, in total control. The bride had become a queen.

Behind her were her maidens of honor, *chicitas* from the pueblo, and family members, equally delighted before the crowd.

The wedding group moved towards their church and priest. Their bodies synchronized rhythmically to Mendelsohn's wedding march. Several boys and girls followed, holding straw baskets filled with red rose petals. As they marched down the street toward holy ground, they sprinkled their guests with flowers.

They all crowded into the church. Alexey signaled to the priest that they were ready. The bride and groom stood solemnly at the altar. The priest gave his blessings. The bride and groom pledged their love and loyalty in sickness or in health.

"Rings, please."

Alexey searched in his pockets. He didn't realize there were so many slits in his new white suit. He found the two gold bands and gave them to Juanito.

The priest recited the vows and declared "I now pronounce you man and wife."

Florita and Juanito exchanged rings and kissed. Mendelssohn's music rang louder, and cameras flashed throughout the church and into opened doors toward pueblo square.

Cheers of "Congratulations! *Bravo! Olé!* And at that signal, the musicians player louder as they paraded through the streets. Everyone danced. Delighted, hombres threw their sombreros to the sky while ladies with castanets danced Flamenco-style.

"*Olé! Olé! Olé!*" Florita yelled while joining them in the square, and the bride raised her wedding dress higher so she could dance faster.

Alexey was eager to join the crowd and dance with Laryssa, but she was nowhere near. Searching for her, he bumped into several groups of people dancing. He wasn't aware that he was losing his balance because he was beginning to feel drunk.

He continued walking the entire length of the square, searching for her. Not steady on his feet, he entered the church and almost tripped over the front steps that were hidden in darkness. Unable to see clearly, he remembered the church was built with only one small window above the center altar to maintain a constant coolness of air. Squinting and rather dizzy, he groped his way to the rear, fumbling over a row of chairs.

He smelled something sweet, a soft touch of perfume like roses in the spring. He breathed in deeply, and remembered . . .

Following its trail, the scent led him to a confessional stall. Inside, hidden behind the curtain, he saw a tall shadowy figure. The flame from a candle lit a corner where a woman was bent forward. He recognized the red curls and crown of roses in her hair.

Next to her, was a short man, strongly built, twice her width, leaning toward her as if he was in submission or prayer. His face was shadowed by the candle's flame. Only a dark cap in the style of Che Guevara's was visible.

Alexey moved closer and hid behind the curtain. He saw her hands holding several papers. The candle's flame exposed lists of names. He recognized her handwriting. The man wearing the cap took the papers, stuffed them inside his shirt, and moved to leave. The woman put her hand on his shoulder and leaned nearer, whispering in his ear words that Alexey couldn't hear, but he saw them nod to each other.

Alexey tiptoed away, not wanting to see more. He heard from behind his back, that they, too, were moving slowly, to leave.

Alexey reached the church's open door, quickened his pace, and lost himself in the crowd. The music surprised him from his thoughts as he wondered, while stumbling, who was the man with Laryssa? What papers was she handing him? Why?

Alexey looked up as he smelled the scent of roses and saw Laryssa running towards him. She waved, smiled, moved close, kissed him on the cheek, and whispered, "I've been looking for you. Let's dance."

He stared into her eyes which appeared more narrow than he remembered. Her tall body stood erect like a statue of marble, cold and hard.

He tried to turn away, but she pulled him closer and kissed his neck. She wanted him to believe she meant it. And he wanted to believe even more that she meant it.

She sensed his tightness when he moved away. To distract him, or attract him, she moved next to the musicians and started to dance. Her dress composed of silk scarves moved in a frenzy. She raised her bare arms, and several silk scarves flew away, exposing the top part of her body with only one thin fabric. Porous and fine, the silk veil revealed her breasts.

She began to dance as her thin layer of veils flowed in the air. The people of the pueblo gasped as she moved, not accustomed to see such freedom.

She took off her shoes and threw them to Sybil who was dancing nearby.

Barefoot and free, Laryssa moved closer to the crowd and sang in Spanish, *La cucaracha, la cucaracha, no puedo caminar.* The musicians approached her, surrounding her in a circle as she danced, faster and faster. The crowd cheered, wanting more.

The musicians moved closer and played to her feverish pace. She untied the string around her waist and threw flowers to the crowd. She threw her hat to the ground and danced around it. As the music roared louder, she tossed rose buds that had fallen to her breasts. While raising her arms, the scarves spread apart, like wings, showing her bare skin.

Overcome by her own uninhibited emotions, Laryssa didn't realize her breasts were bare. The audience, however, did notice, and mesmerized, clapped to the beat of her dancing. The musicians played louder. Music filled the square.

She danced on and on as three young men in the audience jumped next to her. The musicians played in a wild frenzy. And in their madness, the sounds evoked desire until the passion of music took Laryssa beyond her limits.

The three young men joined her and with their arms made a chair. Other men from the crowd placed her on top of the chair like a queen on a throne. She continued to sing, raising her arms as her bare breasts swayed in the air.

"Stop!" Alexey yelled to the musicians, as he covered her breasts with his jacket. He took her home while the crowd kept screaming "Bravo!"

* * *

Alexey was drunk. He wasn't sure where he was or even who was with him. Smelling sweet roses next to him, he tried to forget what he had seen in the obscured, dark church. All he wanted to remember was his beautiful Laryssa, dancing, so full of life.

Now in bed, he mumbled in a drunken slur, "L-Laryssa, L-Laryssa, my dancing goddess. W-Where art thou dear maiden?" He smiled, took her in his arms and drew her into bed.

"Here, O Romeo," she laughed. "Your magic has transformed me from a child playing hide-and-seek to a woman of passion."

"I never knew this wild side of you."

"And I never knew this drunken side of you." Laryssa laughed.

"What a day!" Alexey commented, rubbing his brow. "Those Mexicans can really drink."

"And you matched them. Do you remember counting how many tequilas you had?"

"No. My memory is blurred with tequila—blurred. I only remember you were drinking with me before you started to sing. Juanito kept telling you, '*Una màs*—one more.' He wanted you to keep drinking. And you did! The CIA trained you well. You can drink more than anyone I know. Amazing how alcohol brought out another you."

"But you were the winner. You had one more tequila than me and Juanito. '*Una màs*,' he kept telling you, and you did—one more. You kept drinking; you were the winner! I love you drunk," she said, kissing him. "So free."

"And I love you drunk—so mysterious. You were transformed from nightingale to siren. From spy to Circe. You've hypnotized me."

"Do you think our CIA operatives would have recognized us? Both of us, drunk and dancing in a frenzy like Bacchantes in the middle of a Mexican pueblo?"

"No," he confessed. "No one would have believed what passion and music can do."

"I don't want to get out of bed," she announced, snuggling close to him.

"Who said you should—my sleeper agent? Let's go back to sleep and I'll show you how much Romeo loved his Juliet. *Let me count the ways . . .*"

They both laughed.

And Alexey was happy to forget whatever he thought he had remembered.

CHAPTER 21

Chess at the Kremlin with Laryssa as Dealmaker; Yevgeny Prigozhin: Checkmated by the King

---

"Espresso my love?"

"Yes, it might clear my head."

"Good idea, you'll have to concentrate this morning. While you were sleeping, news was in the making. And comments from my drunken genius are needed."

Alexey wondered if she had already read the morning news on her phone.

"First, I was thinking of what you told me the day before the wedding," he reminded her.

"Yes? I hope I haven't forgotten what I said." She tried to rub a headache away from her forehead.

"I'll refresh your memory. About the Ukrainian children being kidnapped. I understand that means a lot to you." Alexey wanted her to absorb that thought and then he'd go on to the next item of the day—about the plane crash.

"You're right," she agreed. "Children being abducted is a crime and all those involved in Russia and Belarus should be punished."

He took her hand and looked into her eyes. "Fresh from your sleep, tell me, apart from securing justice for kidnapped children, what else have you been coordinating with the CIA?"

"There is something else . . ." she admitted, and then hesitated, looking down.

"Yes? Tell me. I need to know everything. I want to have full confidence in you," he reminded her. "Remember, we must be completely open with each other."

She took a deep breath, stared at the sea and beach through the kitchen window, and reflected on how to phrase her words. She had never confided these thoughts to anyone before. She was afraid that Alexey would judge her.

"My mission with the CIA has also been to let Lukashenko believe it's his goal to maintain order in his country and also in the Kremlin for his Russian boss. I think of the ways, strategize the implementation, and Lukashenko takes the credit."

Alexey was concerned. "Lukashenko trusts you?"

"Yes. He believes me and listens to me. We have a history together." She stopped, abruptly. "Working together for twenty years," she added and looked away, afraid that Alexey's jealousy would flare up again. "I have given him some of his best ideas. That's how he gained the confidence of his boss."

She paused again, took a deep breath. Alexey waited. He wondered if she'd say something related to the news about the plane crash.

"I did something recently, with approval from the CIA, which I always do before I plant ideas into Lukashenko's brain . . ." She hesitated again. "I'm responsible . . ."

"About what?" He didn't like the expression on her face.

"Now I'm sorry about what I did . . . it's terrible. Terrible."

"What?" Alexey tried to stay calm. He realized that she had seen the news already from her phone.

"Do you know Prigozhin?" she asked Alexey.

"Of course, the vicious leader of the Wagner group. His soldiers are criminals who were taken out of jail to fight a war. They're all sadistic killers."

"I was the one who brokered the deal that Prigozhin receives immunity from Putin if he stops his mutiny against the Kremlin and goes into exile in Belarus. Lukashenko came to him with the proposal. But I put the idea into his mind." She looked down again, ashamed.

Alexey was surprised. He had expected her to comment on her friend with the Che Guevara cap and confess who he is and what they were scheming. But no—she wanted to talk of the plane crash. He wondered if she was involved in the bomb's explosion?

But no, she wasn't—nor was her little friend. Her mission was to get immunity for Prigozhin. And that's why she had arranged for his plane to go to Minsk from Moscow. The plane that blew up in flames.

Alexey was trying to figure out where her allegiance lay. To help Lukashenko look better in Putin's eyes? But why, if she's working for the CIA? Is she playing both sides? A double agent?

"I made a mistake," Laryssa said, remorsefully. "Maybe Prigozhin should not have gone to Belarus, like I had suggested, but to Africa. He works with leaders there. They would have protected him. I'm responsible for his death."

"No," Alexey responded, trying to comfort her. "The king would have found his pawn anywhere. And checkmated him. Putin wanted to prove that he's the grandmaster. He refused to lose, so he put all the moves on his side! That's why he got rid of Prigozhin. He couldn't trust him anymore."

"How will this all end?" Laryssa felt the two parts of her soul pulling at each other.

Alexey observed her agitation but didn't comment. Then he asked her, "Did you know Prigozhin, personally?"

"Yes, for the past twenty years. He had visited Lukashenko many times to discuss investments. Prigozhin had proposed building up the diamond industry in Minsk. Make our capital compete with Antwerp as Europe's center for diamonds.

"As you know, Prigozhin had control of diamond mines in the Central African Republic. Mines that he had access to. These mines were once owned by the African dictator, Bokassa, who lost power after the affair of the diamond necklace with France's President Giscard d'Estaing."

"I remember that, from 1979. The scandal brought down Giscard and France."

"Yes, but not the African diamond mines. They're richer than ever."

"So, what happened with Prigozhin and his blood diamonds?" Alexey asked.

"Prigozhin got fabulously rich, and negotiated a percentage for Lukashenko to build up Minsk as a diamond center.

"Lukashenko shared this information with Putin; probably to keep himself indispensable. He gave Putin also a good percentage of the deal. That's how Russia strengthened their diamond industry and competed with De Beers. The Russians even put some fake ones in the bucket." They both laughed.

"How did Prigozhin begin his Empire?" Alexey asked, serving her breakfast and answering his own question. "I know he began as an eighteen-year-old in prison. He was caught stealing, even killing, so his mother could put food on the table."

"That's right." Laryssa nodded her head and continued the story. "After nine years in jail, he became even more interested in food. When he was freed, he set up frankfurter stands in St. Petersburg. Successful with this, he partnered with the first grocery chain in St. Petersburg. He then went on to gambling casinos, even had strippers there, and then opened restaurants in St. Petersburg—the boss' hometown. The boss went there often for dinner, brought dignitaries to the restaurant, and then contracted Prigozhin to be his private cook. The boss was afraid of being poisoned. And Prigozhin, the cook, watched over what the king was eating. He became the royal taster."

"Yes, afraid to be poisoned . . ." Alexey stopped talking while pacing the room. Then commented, "Don't forget that Prigozhin's catering company grew into another major enterprise, the Concord Group, which supplies school children, government workers, and the Russian army with meals. The Russian government gave Prigozhin a contract for more than $1 billion in 2022 for one year of service from the Concord catering company, and another billion for his mercenaries, the Wagner Group. And a few billion extra for Prigozhin to start his empire."

Alexey hesitated and then added, "I'm thinking of something else . . . It reminds me of the US investigation of Russian oligarchs. My job at the CIA was to investigate the Concord Group.

"I found lists of coded numbers representing secret VIP members of the group. Upon further investigating, I was able to align the coded numbers to the names of thirty members, including Russian generals and high officials.

"I got these records, supposedly secretly, but now I think they were intentionally planted so the CIA would find them, and somehow make it known to the Kremlin that we had them. Then Putin would have proof of financial malfeasance against thirty of its VIP members. And proof against Prigozhin, too. There'd be a paper trail based on the records we had found. Through Russia's spy agency, they located our records, and the boss shared it with the Russian press. That was Putin's proof to start eliminating some of the traitors, like Prigozhin.

"Perhaps they're the same thirty who helped Prigozhin plan his mutiny against Putin. The cook needed support in his kitchen," Alexey concluded. "Now, there's a lot of generals in the cooking pot for the Kremlin to boil and get rid of. Putin doesn't like to be cut out of deals. Some people say he demands as much as 50% of all business transactions in Russia."

Laryssa added, "A name that comes up often with Prigozhin is Viktor Bout, a Russian arms dealer who was traded for the US basketball player

Brittney Griner in December, 2022. But he's one person who Putin needs, especially now. He wouldn't touch him.

"Exactly," said Alexey. "Bout is nicknamed the Merchant of Death, for being Russia's number one war merchant. He buys arms for the Russians. Viktor Bout and Prigozhin are good friends. They took a trip together recently to Ulyanovsk in central Russia. Wagner soldiers were recuperating there and Prigozhin was handing out medals to them.

"Prigozhin gave an interview to the Russian Press claiming that Viktor Bout was the smartest person he knew. He praised him for his self-education while in an American prison, learning many languages, including Farsi."

Alexey stopped talking, and took a deep breath and stared at Laryssa. "Farsi is the Iranian language. He's probably negotiating directly with the Iranians about supplying Russia with Shahed drones to use against Ukraine."

Alexey took out his cell phone and texted a message to investigate Bout on that matter. Then he returned his attention back to Laryssa.

"Prigozhin told the press that Viktor Bout is handling all weapons deliveries for Russia." Alexey shrugged his shoulders, disgusted with the intrigues. "Putin needs him for this war. That's why he traded him for Brittney Griner."

Alexey continued talking. "Tell me, do you know what type of man this Prigozhin was?"

"A criminal of no morals," she replied. "He obeyed no one, executing his power with heinous crimes and sadistic games. His soldiers had to call him 'Number One,' not Prigozhin, or they'd find themselves at the front line of battle. Prigozhin was the gatekeeper of hell."

Alexey made a grimace of disgust. "I had heard that he was in remission for stomach cancer. Yet, he continued to be useful."

Laryssa looked down, ashamed that she had been involved with Prigozhin. "Useful but not indispensable."

"Regarding indispensable," Alexey commented. "I wonder if Lukashenko and Bashar al-Assad are also indispensable to Putin."

"Are you talking about Assad of Syria?"

"Yes."

"What do you mean?" Laryssa asked.

"According to the Financial Times, Bashar al-Assad secretly transported $250 million in $100 bills and 500-euro banknotes from Syria's Central Bank to TsMR Bank in Moscow and to the Russian Financial Corporation that deals in arms between March 2018 and September 2019."

"How did he do that?"

"Assad used twenty-one air flights at night, comprised of firefighting helicopters that had Bambi buckets attached to the helicopter. The buckets can carry large weights in the air. And they did, for several weeks, but not containing water. The buckets were filled with medicines and food, so-called for humanitarian aid. But all of Assad's stolen cash and gold was at the bottom of the bucket—two tons with each flight."

"What's a Bambi bucket?"

"It's a bucket that mechanically can scoop up water and then when the pilot releases a valve, the bucket drops the water on a wildfire. The bucket is attached to a long-wired cable from the helicopter's tailgate section. Assad used a Karmov KA-32 model, a Russian design. It's the preferred helicopter of Iran's Revolutionary Guard, built to deliver heavy equipment in secret, like bombs or drones, or even gold bars. Its advantage is that it can take off and land on unpaved ground, like mountains and desert. The helicopter is also equipped with special guiding lights that can't be detected from the exterior or picked up on radar or aviation security."

"Why did Assad escape to Russia with all his money?"

"Russia is a friendly country for him with no extradition laws. Since 2013, Assad has been buying luxury apartments in Moscow. Now he has more than twenty apartments, other investments, and more than a billion dollars to live on there."

"Why did Putin allow this?"

"Putin's payback and a deal. Russia has a large port in Syria, the Tartus Naval Base. It opens up to the Mediterranean. It's Russia's warm water port that allows trade to the Black Sea, Turkey and Africa. Putin needs that port for his nuclear warships and submarines. And he needs Assad's protection, even now, to keep the harbor safe."

CHAPTER 22

Suicide or Homicide: A Warning; Pegasus Spyware Revisited; Plan "A"

"Tell me," Laryssa asked Alexey while getting dressed. "How did you work with our friend, Vlad, while you were living in Washington?"

"That was complicated, but not impossible. Vlad came in every few months on official business as the foreign minister for Lukashenko. No one in the dictator's sphere had ever suspected anything but loyalty from Vlad.

"Yet, once he finished his diplomatic business by day, he'd return to his hotel and become a double agent by night.

"He'd mess up his bed and bathroom, leave his dirty clothes on the floor, and then as soon as it was dark, he'd sneak out of the hotel from the basement that led to a secret alley. He'd take a cab to my house. All cloaked in mystery.

"We'd have dinner together and spend the night talking strategy until early morning. Before the sun would rise, he'd leave to return to his hotel through the same alley and basement and then order room service for breakfast and continue his official day."

"Amazing," she said. "Like a chapter from a spy thriller. And no one ever knew. Not even me."

"But you must have heard us toast you? The first thing we did before we had dinner was to raise our glass of wine to our beautiful comrade, Laryssa."

She pulled his ear and smiled.

Alexey looked down. His mood turned sober as he thought of his best friend, no longer with them. "When I heard about Vlad's death two days after Thanksgiving, I was here in Mexico. There's an Orthodox church near

Tulum. I haven't been into a church since my father died. I stayed there for hours and prayed."

"Vlad was my hero," she murmured and wiped tears from her cheeks. "He truly tried to bridge the West and East. He even tried to have Belarus and China broker a peace deal for the war."

"Ah! China as the deal maker," Alexey said, laughing and picked up Laryssa, swinging her in the air. "America's way to make a bargain with the devil. Economics for peace. Money! Money! Money!"

They both stared at each other, realizing that their thoughts were not a game: Russia, Belarus, and China were all working with America on silent deals. Like double agent spies.

* * *

"How much longer can you stay with me?" he asked her as they were eating breakfast.

"I hope to be with you for a very long time," she answered, taking his hand. "I've notified Nikky that Sybil needs me to stay longer with her."

"Let's review Vlad's plan for democracy," he began, as he put on the espresso machine for more coffee.

"Do you want anything else for breakfast?" he asked her.

"No, this is fine."

Alexey took out several sheets of paper. "Remnants of our student days. I still like to write by hand when I'm reflecting. Then we'll memorize everything and rip up our papers. Like we did as students." He gave her several sheets of paper and a pen.

"While you were sleeping, dear sleeping beauty, I was coordinating with our group in Minsk, Kyiv, and Washington about the details of this operation. This is what we all agreed to do for Plan A.

"First, you and I stay here at my house in Tulum until tomorrow night, and then together we'll go to Washington. Let me communicate this schedule to my assistant in Minsk."

"Wait!" she said, taking his cell phone from his hand.

"What's the matter? It's my Blackberry, a new model." He stared at her as she pressed several buttons from his text messages.

"What are you doing?"

"I want to check if you're being surveilled."

"Surveilled? It's a special Blackberry approved by the Mossad for its security capability and used by operatives to send sensitive, coded messages. I use it often."

"But it's not trustworthy, anywhere, especially in Mexico. In Mexico," she repeated and showed him a red light that was flashing on his text. Then she read to him the message: "Blackberry believes you are being targeted by state-sponsored hackers."

"What's this!" Alexey said, raising his voice. "That's never happened before!"

"This is Pegasus updated. Nikky explained it to me. That's one of the reasons why he has an appointment with the Mexican military, to discuss the abusive use of this spyware.

"Pegasus is the number one spying software, made by a private cyber-intelligence Israeli firm and sold to the Mexican military in 2011. They were their first client, supposedly to use it against narcotics agents. But now they use it against students who demonstrate against the right-wing government.

"Israel uses it in their cyber-attacks. They even use it with AI to locate where their hostages are hidden.

"Apple is working to sue Pegasus out of its existence. Legally, no government should be using it. But, Mexico and their military, without telling any foreign government, continue on. That's why Nikky knows about it.

"Pegasus is illegal," she repeated. "And yet, it's still being used abusively, even in India. It's the most sophisticated spy tool ever created."

"I'll have to be careful," Alexey commented, putting it in his pocket.

After Alexey used his message machine in his closet, he explained to her what he had texted. "I've arranged the safety of your daughters and father through my chief assistant in Minsk, who will visit them in one hour at your apartment—evening there. He'll drive the three of them to the Lithuanian border and from there to a nearby military post.

"It'll take him two hours to drive from Minsk to Lithuania. It's a question of quick action, because at midnight, all the borders of Belarus with Lithuania, Latvia, and Poland will be closed.

"I'm using a subterfuge tonight just in case midnight comes more quickly in Lithuania."

"What is it?" She was concerned for her daughters.

"My assistant will use an ambulance from *Les Médecins Sans Frontières*. He'll arrange for the girls to get dressed as nurses and your father as a doctor.

Once in Lithuania, he'll escort them to a military plane for Washington. And from there, to my house. They'll wait for us there."

He paused so she could approve of what he was planning, which she did with a nod. "Can all this be done before midnight?" she asked, worried.

"Yes. Once we're all together in the States, I'll submit papers for your daughters for student visas, so they can stay in Washington until I can get them green cards. We'll enroll them as students."

"They'll be surprised. They never knew about my work."

"They'll soon find out. My assistant will explain everything to them as they drive to the Lithuanian border," he explained.

"First, you should contact your daughters and father and speak to them in an indirect way so no one else can understand. Prepare them."

She nodded again. "My priority is that my family is safe. You promise me that? No matter what happens to me, you'll protect them? Promise me?"

He found her question odd, and her insistence on the matter even stranger. "Of course. I promise."

She took his hand and shook it. "Agreed. And next?"

"Next is your general. I'll notify him by code that you're here with me." Alexey smiled. "I'll put in a P.S. that Laryssa is very safe with me."

"I wonder if he'll be surprised. Or do you think he expects it? Did you or someone from your group inform him?"

"No, how could I? I didn't know myself that you were here. In my arms, my beautiful señorita."

Alexey turned serious. In a whisper he told Laryssa, "I've received news from my enquiries about Nikky. He's not to be trusted. He works with his Russian cousin, who organized the terrorist scares against us in the pueblo. Nikky has shared with him information about you.

"Have you suspected any attempted violence against you from Nikky?" Alexey stared hard at her.

"Well, yes and no. I guess more yes than no. First, a car aimed at me near Central Park. I ran away. And then also at home in New York, with Nikky. It started with his drunken violence. I told you about that."

She saw Alexey was getting angry.

"But I handled Nikky," she reassured him.

"From now on," Alexey insisted, "I'll handle Nikky, and he'll follow my orders. He doesn't expect anything, yet. I'll trap him into thinking he can trust me and get more information from me."

"You'll trap him? You must be good at that." She gave him a strange grin.

He gave her a wink and nod of the head. "I'll get Nikky to my house tomorrow evening. I'll take him for a walk on the beach, to 'discuss strategy.' He'll be concentrating on my ideas so he can share them with his group, and that's when I'll have my men arrest him."

"And what's the plan for me?" Laryssa asked, staring at him, slightly suspiciously.

"After dinner, you'll leave with me from here. The weather will be good for our escape. Rain will begin in the early evening and last throughout the night. There'll be fog without a moon. A sea plane with silent engines will land directly on my beach after the CIA and I arrest Nikky. The plane will take us both to Washington, D.C. The day after tomorrow, we'll be united in Washington with Tanya, Clara and your father."

"And then?" she asked him.

"From Washington, you and I will join a selected group of US troops, as well as with volunteer soldiers from European countries, to go to Minsk and overtake the capital. The soldiers will begin demonstrations there and let ordinary citizens cause havoc. We'll intersperse ourselves into the crowd with the CIA who will stage a coup d'état against the dictator.

"Our network will begin with riot techniques, like smoke bombs, water pellets, and Molotov cocktails. We'll cause havoc but no violence.

"The Belarusian army will automatically be sent to Minsk by Lukashenko to make arrests. At that moment, a special American Green Béret unit and NATO soldiers will arrest Lukashenko and force him to step down."

"That's very optimistic. I would even say, naïve. He's not the type to give up or lose. He'll never relinquish control. Maybe you should try to work with him instead, in a way to get his confidence. Offer him more than what the Russians offer him—total immunity with big bucks and a lifetime of safety."

"No, my love! I'd rather offer him a bullet through his head. He does what I say or . . ."

Alexey stood up and took from his kitchen cabinet a long automatic rifle. "This has the capacity to shoot twenty shots in twenty seconds. He'll recognize the rifle. He approved it himself. But he won't want it used on him."

Laryssa stared at the rifle as Alexey returned it to the cabinet. He moved towards her and put his arms around her. "Laryssa, my love, we had promised each other when we were students that we'd try to help our people."

She looked at Alexey in his eyes and took his hand. "I still feel the same way. But I want to do it in a way never done before."

CHAPTER 23

Plan "B"; Love Stops Time; Miracles do Happen

Alexey led Laryssa toward the dunes on the beach. "Let's walk and consider Viktor's plan B. He suggested that we stay in Washington to help prepare a peace treaty. He said a cease-fire is needed, as well as guarantees for territories."

"You mean which country will get the land they captured during the war. Especially the northeast."

"That'll be the stumbling block," Alexey replied, shrugging his shoulders. "Russia thinks it's all theirs."

"A peace treaty means compromises." Laryssa picked up a handful of sand and threw it hard. "And we can't let Belarus become a permanent vassal state of Russia."

Alexey agreed, kicking sand as they walked. "Putin has stationed nuclear weapons on Belarus' border. He probably plans to use Belarus to attack a NATO country."

"Who would have imagined that Europe's future stability could be rooted in our small country." She paused, as the idea made her angry.

"What can we do?"

"Play a game," she quickly answered. "I believe in playing Russian Roulette. It entails a lack of control—allowing fate to make decisions, and yet, it gives you extreme control—to face death willingly." She stared at him and said emphatically, "That's life."

Alexey took Laryssa's hand. "I understand. But if we play Russian Roulette, we have to be highly secretive."

"Trust me. I know a way."

He looked at her, rather surprised. "I'm trying to find something good from all of this."

"Our love story," she stated and kissed him. "How about we celebrate that with a festive dinner. It'll be our last evening here."

"Good idea. We'll act as if it's an ordinary evening. And then late at night, we'll secretly board our sea plane."

"I'll invite our friends, Sybil, Gene, James, and Hildie."

***

"What a great idea," Sybil responded to the invitation for dinner at the beach. "I was just going to knock on your door and invite you and Alexey to join us tonight. But I was reluctant to bother you both." She smiled, realizing that they were happy to be alone.

"Gene and I went fishing this morning," Sybil commented. "We got twelve Bonitos. I gave half to my brother's gardener, but we've plenty left over for dinner tonight for all of us. James can grill them. Make life simple."

"Simple?" Laryssa smiled. "I wish it were."

Then, unexpectedly, Laryssa took Sybil in her arms and whispered, "Thank you for what you have given me and for doing it so kindly."

Sybil gave her a puzzled look. "What do you mean?"

"You gave me back Alexey."

Taking Laryssa's hand, Sybil explained why. "I felt your sadness, despite your stoic front. I felt there was something inside you that was empty. A lost love that you were searching for. So, I grabbed the chance to do something decent. All I did was to take fate and help it go towards you. Love has the power to reward the good. And I felt the good in you."

Laryssa smiled. "Tell me, Sybil, did you spy on me to learn this?"

"Yes. How did you know?"

"My dear, you're a writer. You have to spy to collect fragments of truth. You once told me that a writer's memory is a treasure chest. And in your magic box you've stored fragments of people you've met to make your story true."

"Yes, mysteriously, people and scenes take shape in my mind, without my knowing why or how. Sometimes, I marvel that the imaginary can merge into reality, and they become one. Just as it happened with you, Laryssa.

"Let me confess, this novel has been a voyage—your voyage to find your love again. And by loving, you've found a reason to live—a reason that both of you will share. That, my friend, is a miracle!"

* * *

James and Gene were busy grilling the fish. Hildie and Laryssa were preparing a salad. Sybil was cleaning some corn.

Alexey appeared on the beach, waving to the group. He gave Laryssa a nod and wink.

"My best wine," he announced, walking towards them and holding up two bottles. "Sorry I'm late. Took me some time to choose the wine. Our dinner deserves a good year."

He smiled with his secret and looked up at the clouds. "Looks like it might rain." He tried to appear displeased, but a foggy exit is exactly what he wanted.

"Not until later," James commented. "Let's start dinner outside and then we'll see if it rains."

Sybil stopped setting the table to look at the sky. "I hope it clears by tomorrow. We're taking a plane back to New York. Vacation is over."

"Don't worry," James reassured her. "The weather will clear by morning."

Laryssa caught Alexey's eye to make sure all was going as planned. He gave her a private thumbs-up.

Gene carried a tray of cheese and crackers and set them on the table next to several bowls of *ceviche*. "Look at you two," Gene said to Alexey and Laryssa. "You look so dressed up. Alexey, why are you wearing a white shirt and slacks? And you, Laryssa, wearing makeup? I feel so awkward in my bathing suit and T-shirt."

"Looks like you're ready for a city party," James commented, "or something special."

Laryssa quickly replied, "This is special. All of us being together with the catch of the day."

Alexey, to avoid explaining why they weren't dressed in beach clothes, spoke instead of the wine. "Tell me if this vintage is good enough for our celebration." And he raised his glass first to Laryssa, and then to his friends.

"James," Alexey said, turning to him. "I was thinking that you don't have the keys to my house. In case you ever need them."

James looked slightly surprised. "Why would I need them?"

"You never know what tomorrow brings. Just in case, here." Alexey gave him a spare set.

"Not a bad idea. I'll get mine for you tomorrow."

They all sat down to enjoy the ceviche. Hildie commented that the gardener's wife had prepared it for them. "Susanna made it from the Bonito."

James brought the grilled fish to the table and bowed as there were murmurs of "compliments to the chef!"

Alexey was busy chatting. Laryssa was quiet. They tried to hide their nervousness, each in their own way.

James turned to Sybil and raised his glass. "To my sister. May she forget the days of our youth—our fights with each other and our fights to survive. We've paid our price to life and now we toast the future."

"Peace," Sybil agreed.

Alexey raised his glass to Laryssa. "To our choices, as we, too, had to survive."

Hildie took her glass and to everyone at the table, raised it, "To all of us. Survivors from different countries. Each one in our own way."

They chatted and laughed, enjoying being together. A vacation on the beach had been special for all of them.

Hildie looked at the sky and commented, "I feel a breeze. Look at the palm trees, starting to blow. Wind is coming and maybe rain. Do you think we should go inside?"

"Yes," answered Gene as he picked up some plates and bowls. "I feel some drops."

Hildie looked at her watch. "Perfect timing. The ten o'clock news is on. I want to hear what they say about Ukraine."

"Let's hear tonight's update from Kyiv," James agreed, taking the last of the dishes from the table.

Alexey looked at Laryssa, nodded his head, and said, "How about a stroll on the beach. Actually, the beach is quite beautiful surrounded by mist and fog."

"Yes," she agreed. "Looks like a mystery."

Laryssa turned to him, put her arm through his to leave and said goodbye first to Sybil.

"My dear friend, I'll phone you in the morning to discuss the latest news." Then she kissed everyone goodnight.

Alexey took Laryssa's hand, and they walked to the far end of the beach.

CHAPTER 24

Separate Ways, Together

Alexey felt a vibration at his hip from his Blackberry. He glanced at the message and told Laryssa, "The sea plane is delayed because of fog. Let me see when the pilot thinks the fog will lift."

He walked alone to the far end of the beach to answer his call.

"The delay isn't because of the fog," the pilot explained. "I received word from headquarters that there's a private coded message for you to read immediately. I'll circle a few minutes to give you time to retrieve it. Then we'll communicate what to do."

Alexey punched in his secret code to his Blackberry. A photo of the dark inside of the church from the wedding appeared on the screen. Then followed was a photo of several white papers. A woman's hand passed the pages to a man who was bent down. Alexey recognized the woman's red nail polish. The man's cap fell to the ground. He picked it up and placed the papers in his shirt.

Then another photo appeared on the cell phone screen with magnified copies of the three pages. On the first page was a list of prisoner names to be freed from Belarus' main jail. On the next page was a much longer list of Belarusian people to be arrested. On the third page was a memo: Abort plans to take female partner with you to Washington. Take the plane alone. We will send another plane to return her to Belarus.

Alexey sat down on the sand to think. What did this mean? Should he trust Laryssa? Who was she working for? And if she were to return to Belarus, wasn't it possible that she could get killed?

Alexey walked slowly towards her. He remembered the church, the confessional stall. He saw before him the image of her secret meeting with an unknown man. Her handing him the papers that were now clearly enlarged on his Blackberry screen. The message from Headquarters was precise: Don't take her to Washington.

Several thoughts rushed through his mind. He should have acted at the wedding to confront her, but he couldn't believe it. Easier for him to blame his hesitation on being drunk.

Now clearer in his thoughts, he knew he'd have to solve the problem before taking the plane.

Laryssa approached him. "Is there a problem?"

"Yes." He showed her the first page—the photo of her in the church and the man with the cap.

"Do you know him?"

"Yes. He's my assistant."

"Assistant?"

"Yes, an agent from the CIA."

"Why didn't I know about this? Why wasn't I informed?"

"This has been planned for months before Mexico, before we found each other."

He moved away. She grabbed his arm. "Listen to me. I'm going to tell you the truth and it's imperative that you believe me.

"First and foremost, my allegiance lies with the US. I work for the CIA because I want to help America. I believe in democracy. But there's a ploy I will play. And it's a ploy supported by the CIA."

He stared hard at her.

"I'll return to Belarus, not go with you to Washington."

"I'll prop up Lukashenko to become the backchannel for the US and Russia. Everyone will think it's Lukashenko's idea, his doing. But it will be me, like a fly whispering in his ear, telling him what to say, what to do."

"What does this entail?"

"Lukashenko, parroting my ideas, will gain the trust of the US government by being the go-between, the secret intermediary and building the groundwork for peace. Moscow will agree. They're getting weak. And they've been using Lukashenko for years as their middleman.

"I'll arrange high profile prisoner releases, including several American citizens, using my contacts at the UN, the Pentagon, and the Kremin. I speak the three languages fluently—English, Russian, Belarusian. I've lived in all three countries and understand their culture. Above all, I can guide the Americans to understand how to deal with Lukashenko's ego and to deal with him without emotions. Diplomacy doesn't work with emotion."

Alexey listened. He knew she had guided Lukashenko on several political agendas. Conflict resolution was her strength. She had been working with Lukashenko for more than twenty years in his multi-vector foreign policies.

"What will you get for all this? Will Lukashenko give you a treaty deal with the Emirates or Saudi Arabia, so you'd get a hefty kickback from them? Who will make the deposits in Switzerland for you? The man in the Che Guevara cap?"

Laryssa shook her head no. "Alexey, restrain from emotion. Forget your pride. I can help make peace. That's more important than money. I can get trust from all sides. Lukashenko will step down soon. He's sick. He's getting weak. He'll retire to his Sochi estate.

"The CIA can stage a coup d'etat to take over Belarus, or they can allow me to set-up free elections. Usher in Democracy."

"You think you can do that?"

"Yes. I've already had results with an important prisoner exchange—a VIP American woman. I got her out of prison, to Lithuania, and to the States. All with the presence of the American secretary of state next to us.

"I've proven myself. And I can facilitate more releases. Belarus has the largest number of political prisoners than any country in Europe. I can help get hundreds of people home and let everyone think it's Lukashenko's doing. Appease the Americans. Get good PR."

Alexey felt a vibration at his hip. His Blackberry wanted his attention. "Let me take this," he said to Laryssa, and walked away.

"Chief, let me know when you want me," the pilot reminded Alexey.

"Do you have the backup plane nearby? Can it get here in ten minutes?"

"Yes."

"OK. Send the backup sea plane first and then the next one for me."

Alexey returned to Laryssa. "It's arranged. You'll take the first plane east, to Minsk. I'll take the second plane west, to Washington."

She took his hand. "Alexey. I truly love you. With all my heart and soul. Trust me to do what's right. I've had the chance to infiltrate into the three governments—and in secret."

"A secret from me, too," he said sarcastically.

"Yes, and still secret. That's what will keep us together. The secret will bind us."

He took her in his arms. "Agreed. Remember, I will always love you."

"And I will always love you."

***

Upon arriving in Washington the next day, Alexey's car met him at the tarmac. He entered the limo's back seat, turned on his Blackberry, programmed it to scan the main square in Minsk.

He saw Laryssa standing on a platform with a microphone in her hand. Surrounding her were crowds of thousands of young people waving Belarusian flags and shouting her name.

Behind Laryssa, he noticed the university where they had fallen in love. Next to the building was the bistro where Vlad had played the piano while Laryssa sang American songs.

Now, she was telling students to unite for Democracy. Make way for Freedom.

Alexey breathed in deeply, relieved that she was safe.

He smiled, imagining he could smell roses in the spring.

And he remembered the Cherokee parable:

"There are two wolves inside each person. When asked which wolf wins, an elder replies, 'Whichever one you feed.'"

THE END

www.ingramcontent.com/pod-product-compliance
Lightning Source LLC
LaVergne TN
LVHW011656100826
845155LV00004B/13

9798887198941